Tuck
Everlasting

with
Connections

Tuck Everlasting

N A T A L I E   B A B B I T T

with
Connections

HOLT, RINEHART AND WINSTON
Harcourt Brace & Company

Austin • New York • Orlando • Atlanta • San Francisco
Boston • Dallas • Toronto • London

For permission to reprint copyrighted material, grateful acknowledgment is made to the following sources:

Farrar, Straus & Giroux, Inc.: *Tuck Everlasting* by Natalie Babbitt. Copyright © 1975 by Natalie Babbitt. All rights reserved.

Don Congdon Associates, Inc.: "Hail and Farewell" by Ray Bradbury from *Today,* March 29, 1953. Copyright © 1953 and renewed © 1981 by Ray Bradbury. *David Higham Associates Limited:* "The Return of Oisin" from *The High Deeds of Finn MacCool* by Rosemary Sutcliff. Copyright © 1967 by Rosemary Sutcliff. *Pantheon Books, a division of Random House, Inc.:* "Coyote and the Origin of Death" and "The End of the World" from *American Indian Myths and Legends,* edited by Richard Erdoes and Alfonso Ortiz. Copyright © 1984 by Richard Erdoes and Alfonso Ortiz. *Random House UK Ltd.:* Text from *How to Live Forever* by Colin Thompson. Copyright © 1995 by Colin Thompson. *Charles E. Tuttle Company, Inc., Rutland, Vermont and Tokyo, Japan:* "Hakusai" (retitled "Farewell") by Hakusai and untitled poem (retitled "I Thought to Live") by Hanabusa Ikkei, English and Japanese versions, from *Japanese Death Poems* by Zen Monks and Haiku Poets on the Verge of Death, compiled by Yoel Hoffmann. Copyright © 1986 by Charles E. Tuttle Company, Inc. *University of Oklahoma Press:* "Old Man and Old Woman," (retitled "It Is Better To Die Forever") retold by Chewing Blackbones from *Indian Legends from the Northern Rockies* by Ella E. Clark. Copyright © 1966 by the University of Oklahoma Press.

Cover photographs: (tree background) Michael Orton/Tony Stone; (eyes) Victoria Smith/ HRW Photo   .

HRW is a registered trademark licensed to Holt, Rinehart and Winston.

Printed in the United States of America
ISBN 0-03-054783-0

56 043 02 01

Contents

Prologue

The first week of August hangs at the very top of summer, the top of the live-long year, like the highest seat of a Ferris wheel when it pauses in its turning. The weeks that come before are only a climb from balmy spring, and those that follow a drop to the chill of autumn, but the first week of August is motionless, and hot. It is curiously silent, too, with blank white dawns and glaring noons, and sunsets smeared with too much color. Often at night there is lightning, but it quivers all alone. There is no thunder, no relieving rain. These are strange and breathless days, the dog days, when people are led to do things they are sure to be sorry for after.

One day at that time, not so very long ago, three things happened and at first there appeared to be no connection between them.

At dawn, Mae Tuck set out on her horse for the wood at the edge of the village of Treegap. She was going there, as she did once every ten years, to meet her two sons, Miles and Jesse.

At noontime, Winnie Foster, whose family owned the Treegap wood, lost her patience at last and decided to think about running away.

And at sunset a stranger appeared at the Fosters' gate. He was looking for someone, but he didn't say who.

No connection, you would agree. But things can come together in strange ways. The wood was at the center, the hub of the wheel. All wheels must have a hub. A Ferris wheel has one, as the sun is the hub of the wheeling calendar. Fixed points they are, and best left undisturbed, for without them, nothing holds together. But sometimes people find this out too late.

1

The road that led to Treegap had been trod out long before by a herd of cows who were, to say the least, relaxed. It wandered along in curves and easy angles, swayed off and up in a pleasant tangent to the top of a small hill, ambled down again between fringes of bee-hung clover, and then cut sidewise across a meadow. Here its edges blurred. It widened and seemed to pause, suggesting tranquil bovine picnics: slow chewing and thoughtful contemplation of the infinite. And then it went on again and came at last to the wood. But on reaching the shadows of the first trees, it veered sharply, swung out in a wide arc as if, for the first time, it had reason to think where it was going, and passed around.

On the other side of the wood, the sense of easiness dissolved. The road no longer belonged to the cows. It became, instead, and rather abruptly, the property of people. And all at once the sun was uncomfortably hot, the dust oppressive, and the meager grass along its edges somewhat ragged and forlorn. On the left stood the first house, a square and solid cottage with a touch-me-not appearance, surrounded by grass cut painfully to the quick and enclosed by a capable iron fence some four feet high which clearly said, "Move on—we don't want *you* here." So the road went humbly by and made its way, past cottages more and more frequent but less and less forbidding, into the village. But the village doesn't matter, except for the jailhouse and the gallows. The first house only is important; the first house, the road, and the wood.

There was something strange about the wood. If the look of the first house suggested that you'd better pass it by, so did the look of the wood, but for quite a different reason. The house was so proud of itself that you wanted to make a lot of noise as you passed, and maybe even throw a rock or two. But the wood had a sleeping, otherworld appearance that made you want to speak in whispers. This, at least, is what the cows must have thought: "Let it keep its peace; *we* won't disturb it."

Whether the people felt that way about the wood or not is difficult to say. There were some, perhaps, who did. But for the most part the people followed the road around the wood because that was the way it led. There was no road *through* the wood. And anyway, for the people, there was another reason to leave the wood to itself: it belonged to the Fosters, the owners of the touch-me-not cottage, and was therefore private property in spite of the fact that it lay outside the fence and was perfectly accessible.

The ownership of land is an odd thing when you come to think of it. How deep, after all, can it go? If a person owns a piece of land, does he own it all the way down, in ever narrowing dimensions, till it meets all other pieces at the center of the earth? Or does ownership consist only of a thin crust under which the friendly worms have never heard of trespassing?

In any case, the wood, being on top—except, of course, for its roots—was owned bud and bough by the Fosters in the touch-me-not cottage, and if they never went there, if they never wandered in among the trees, well, that was their affair. Winnie, the only child of the house, never went there, though she sometimes stood inside the fence, carelessly banging a stick against the iron bars, and looked at it. But she had never been curious about it. Nothing ever seems interesting when it belongs to you—only when it doesn't.

And what is interesting, anyway, about a slim few acres of trees? There will be a dimness shot through with bars of sunlight, a great many squirrels and birds, a deep, damp mattress of leaves on the ground, and all the other things just as familiar if not so pleasant—things like spiders, thorns, and grubs.

In the end, however, it was the cows who were responsible for the wood's isolation, and the cows, through some wisdom they were not wise enough to know that they possessed, were very wise indeed. If they had made their road through the wood instead of around it, then the people would have followed the road. The people would have noticed the giant ash tree at the center of the wood, and then, in time, they'd have noticed the little spring bubbling up among its roots in spite of the pebbles piled there to conceal it. And that would have been a disaster so immense that this weary old earth, owned or not to its fiery core, would have trembled on its axis like a beetle on a pin.

2

And so, at dawn, that day in the first week of August, Mae Tuck woke up and lay for a while beaming at the cobwebs on the ceiling. At last she said aloud, "The boys'll be home tomorrow!"

Mae's husband, on his back beside her, did not stir. He was still asleep, and the melancholy creases that folded his daytime face were smoothed and slack. He snored gently, and for a moment the corners of his mouth turned upward in a smile. Tuck almost never smiled except in sleep.

Mae sat up in bed and looked at him tolerantly. "The boys'll be home tomorrow," she said again, a little more loudly.

Tuck twitched and the smile vanished. He opened his eyes. "Why'd you have to wake me up?" he sighed. "I was having that dream again, the good one where we're all in heaven and never heard of Treegap."

Mae sat there frowning, a great potato of a woman with a round, sensible face and calm brown eyes. "It's no use having that dream," she said. "Nothing's going to change."

"You tell me that every day," said Tuck, turning away from her onto his side. "Anyways, I can't help what I dream."

"Maybe not," said Mae. "But, all the same, you should've got used to things by now."

Tuck groaned. "I'm going back to sleep," he said.

"Not me," said Mae. "I'm going to take the horse and go down to the wood to meet them."

"Meet who?"

"The boys, Tuck! Our sons. I'm going to ride down to meet them."

"Better not do that," said Tuck.

"I know," said Mae, "but I just can't wait to see them. Anyways, it's ten years since I went to Treegap. No one'll remember me. I'll ride in at sunset, just to the wood. I won't go into the village. But, even if someone did see me, they won't remember. They never did before, now, did they?"

"Suit yourself, then," said Tuck into his pillow. "I'm going back to sleep."

Mae Tuck climbed out of bed and began to dress: three petticoats, a rusty brown skirt with one enormous pocket, an old cotton jacket, and a knitted shawl which she pinned across her bosom with a tarnished metal brooch. The sounds of her dressing were so familiar to Tuck that he could say, without opening his eyes, "You don't need that shawl in the middle of the summer."

Mae ignored this observation. Instead, she said, "Will you be all right? We won't get back till late tomorrow."

Tuck rolled over and made a rueful face at her. "What in the world could possibly happen to me?"

"That's so," said Mae. "I keep forgetting."

"*I* don't," said Tuck. "Have a nice time." And in a moment he was asleep again.

Mae sat on the edge of the bed and pulled on a pair of short leather boots so thin and soft with age it was a wonder they held together. Then she stood and took from the washstand beside the bed a little square-shaped object, a music box painted with roses and lilies of the valley. It was the one pretty thing she owned and she never went anywhere without it. Her fingers strayed to the winding key on its bottom, but glancing at the sleeping Tuck, she shook her head, gave the little box a pat, and dropped it into her pocket. Then, last of all, she pulled down over her ears a blue straw hat with a drooping, exhausted brim.

But, before she put on the hat, she brushed her

gray-brown hair and wound it into a bun at the back of her neck. She did this quickly and skillfully without a single glance in the mirror. Mae Tuck didn't need a mirror, though she had one propped up on the washstand. She knew very well what she would see in it; her reflection had long since ceased to interest her. For Mae Tuck, and her husband, and Miles and Jesse, too, had all looked exactly the same for eighty-seven years.

3

At noon of that same day in the first week of August, Winnie Foster sat on the bristly grass just inside the fence and said to the large toad who was squatting a few yards away across the road, "I will, though. You'll see. Maybe even first thing tomorrow, while everyone's still asleep."

It was hard to know whether the toad was listening or not. Certainly, Winnie had given it good reason to ignore her. She had come out to the fence, very cross, very near the boiling point on a day that was itself near to boiling, and had noticed the toad at once. It was the only living thing in sight except for a stationary cloud of hysterical gnats suspended in the heat above the road. Winnie had found some pebbles at the base of the fence and, for lack of any other way to show how she felt, had flung one at the toad. It missed altogether, as she'd fully intended it should, but she made a game of it anyway, tossing pebbles at such an angle that they passed through the gnat cloud on their way to the toad. The gnats were too frantic to notice these intrusions, however, and since every pebble missed its final mark, the toad continued to squat and grimace without so much as a twitch. Possibly it felt resentful. Or perhaps it was only asleep. In either case, it gave her not a glance when at last she ran out of pebbles and sat down to tell it her troubles.

"Look here, toad," she said, thrusting her arms through the bars of the fence and plucking at the weeds on the other side. "I don't think I can stand it much longer."

At this moment a window at the front of the cottage was flung open and a thin voice—her grandmother's—piped, "Winifred! Don't sit on that dirty grass. You'll stain your boots and stockings."

And another, firmer voice—her mother's—added, "Come in now, Winnie. Right away. You'll get heat stroke out there on a day like this. And your lunch is ready."

"See?" said Winnie to the toad. "That's just what I mean. It's like that every minute. If I had a sister or a brother, there'd be someone else for them to watch. But, as it is, there's only me. I'm tired of being looked at all the time. I want to be by myself for a change." She leaned her forehead against the bars and after a short silence went on in a thoughtful tone. "I'm not exactly sure what I'd do, you know, but something interesting—something that's all mine. Something that would make some kind of difference in the world. It'd be nice to have a new name, to start with, one that's not all worn out from being called so much. And I might even decide to have a pet. Maybe a big old toad, like you, that I could keep in a nice cage with lots of grass, and . . ."

At this the toad stirred and blinked. It gave a heave of muscles and plopped its heavy mudball of a body a few inches farther away from her.

"I suppose you're right," said Winnie. "Then you'd be just the way I am, now. Why should you have to be cooped up in a cage, too? It'd be better if I could be like you, out in the open and making up my own mind. Do you know they've hardly ever let me out of this yard all by myself? I'll never be able to do anything important if I stay in here like this. I expect I'd better run away." She paused and peered anxiously at the toad to see how it would receive this staggering idea, but it showed no signs of interest. "You think I wouldn't dare, don't you?" she said accusingly. "I will, though. You'll see. Maybe even first thing in the morning, while everyone's still asleep."

"Winnie!" came the firm voice from the window.

"All *right!* I'm coming!" she cried, exasperated, and then added quickly, "I mean, I'll be right there, Mama." She stood up, brushing at her legs where bits of itchy grass clung to her stockings.

The toad, as if it saw that their interview was over, stirred again, bunched up, and bounced itself clumsily off toward the wood. Winnie watched it go. "Hop away, toad," she called after it. "You'll see. Just wait till morning."

4

At sunset of that same long day, a stranger came
strolling up the road from the village and paused at
the Fosters' gate. Winnie was once again in the yard,
this time intent on catching fireflies, and at first she
didn't notice him. But, after a few moments of watching her, he called out, "Good evening!"

He was remarkably tall and narrow, this stranger
standing there. His long chin faded off into a thin,
apologetic beard, but his suit was a jaunty yellow
that seemed to glow a little in the fading light. A
black hat dangled from one hand, and as Winnie
came toward him, he passed the other through his
dry, gray hair, settling it smoothly. "Well, now," he
said in a light voice. "Out for fireflies, are you?"

"Yes," said Winnie.

"A lovely thing to do on a summer evening," said
the man richly. "A lovely entertainment. I used to

do it myself when I was your age. But of course that was a long, long time ago." He laughed, gesturing in self-deprecation with long, thin fingers. His tall body moved continuously; a foot tapped, a shoulder twitched. And it moved in angles, rather jerkily. But at the same time he had a kind of grace, like a well-handled marionette. Indeed, he seemed almost to hang suspended there in the twilight. But Winnie, though she was half charmed, was suddenly reminded of the stiff black ribbons they had hung on the door of the cottage for her grandfather's funeral. She frowned and looked at the man more closely. But his smile seemed perfectly all right, quite agreeable and friendly.

"Is this your house?" asked the man, folding his arms now and leaning against the gate.

"Yes," said Winnie. "Do you want to see my father?"

"Perhaps. In a bit," said the man. "But I'd like to talk to you first. Have you and your family lived here long?"

"Oh, yes," said Winnie. "We've lived here forever."

"Forever," the man echoed thoughtfully.

It was not a question, but Winnie decided to explain anyway. "Well, not forever, of course, but as long as there've been any people here. My grandmother was born here. She says this was all trees once, just one big forest everywhere around, but it's mostly all cut down now. Except for the wood."

"I see," said the man, pulling at his beard. "So of course you know everyone, and everything that goes on."

"Well, not especially," said Winnie. "At least, *I* don't. Why?"

The man lifted his eyebrows. "Oh," he said, "I'm looking for someone. A family."

"I don't know anybody much," said Winnie, with a shrug. "But my father might. You could ask him."

"I believe I shall," said the man. "I do believe I shall."

At this moment the cottage door opened, and in the lamp glow that spilled across the grass, Winnie's grandmother appeared. "Winifred? Who are you talking to out there?"

"It's a man, Granny," she called back. "He says he's looking for someone."

"What's that?" said the old woman. She picked up her skirts and came down the path to the gate. "What did you say he wants?"

The man on the other side of the fence bowed slightly. "Good evening, madam," he said. "How delightful to see you looking so fit."

"And why shouldn't I be fit?" she retorted, peering at him through the fading light. His yellow suit seemed to surprise her, and she squinted suspiciously.

"We haven't met, that I can recall. Who are you? Who are you looking for?"

The man answered neither of these questions. Instead, he said, "This young lady tells me you've lived here for a long time, so I thought you would probably know everyone who comes and goes."

The old woman shook her head. "I *don't* know everyone," she said, "nor do I want to. And I don't stand outside in the dark discussing such a thing with strangers. Neither does Winifred. So . . ."

And then she paused. For, through the twilight sounds of crickets and sighing trees, a faint, surprising wisp of music came floating to them, and all three turned toward it, toward the wood. It was a tinkling little melody, and in a few moments it stopped.

"My stars!" said Winnie's grandmother, her eyes round. "I do believe it's come again, after all these years!" She pressed her wrinkled hands together, forgetting the man in the yellow suit. "Did you hear that, Winifred? That's it! That's the elf music I told you about. Why, it's been ages since I heard it last. And this is the first time you've *ever* heard it, isn't it? Wait till we tell your father!" And she seized Winnie's hand and turned to go back into the cottage.

"Wait!" said the man at the gate. He had stiffened, and his voice was eager. "You've heard that music before, you say?"

But, before he could get an answer, it began again and they all stopped to listen. This time it tinkled its way faintly through the little melody three times before it faded.

"It sounds like a music box," said Winnie when it was over.

"Nonsense. It's elves!" crowed her grandmother excitedly. And then she said to the man at the gate, "You'll have to excuse us now." She shook the gate latch under his nose, to make sure it was locked, and then, taking Winnie by the hand once more, she marched up the path into the cottage, shutting the door firmly behind her.

But the man in the yellow suit stood tapping his foot in the road for a long time all alone, looking at the wood. The last stains of sunset had melted away, and the twilight died, too, as he stood there, though its remnants clung reluctantly to everything that was pale in color—pebbles, the dusty road, the figure of the man himself—turning them blue and blurry.

Then the moon rose. The man came to himself and sighed. His expression was one of intense satisfaction. He put on his hat, and in the moonlight his long fingers were graceful and very white. Then he turned and disappeared down the shadowy road, and as he went he whistled, very softly, the tinkling little melody from the wood.

5

Winnie woke early next morning. The sun was only just opening its own eye on the eastern horizon and the cottage was full of silence. But she realized that sometime during the night she had made up her mind: she would not run away today. "Where would I go, anyway?" she asked herself. "There's nowhere else I really want to be." But in another part of her head, the dark part where her oldest fears were housed, she knew there was another sort of reason for staying at home: she was afraid to go away alone.

It was one thing to talk about being by yourself, doing important things, but quite another when the opportunity arose. The characters in the stories she read always seemed to go off without a thought or care, but in real life—well, the world was a danger-ous place. People were always telling her so. And she would not be able to manage without protection. They were always telling her that, too. No one ever said precisely what it was that she would not be able to manage. But she did not need to ask. Her own imagination supplied the horrors.

Still, it was galling, this having to admit she was afraid. And when she remembered the toad, she felt even more disheartened. What if the toad should be out by the fence again today? What if he should laugh at her secretly and think she was a coward?

Well, anyway, she could at least slip out, right now, she decided, and go into the wood. To see if she could discover what had really made the music the night before. That would be something, anyway. She did not allow herself to consider the idea that making a difference in the world might require a bolder venture. She merely told herself consolingly, "Of course, while I'm in the wood, if I decide never to come back, well then, that will be that." She was able to believe in this because she needed to; and, believing, was her own true, promising friend once more.

It was another heavy morning, already hot and breathless, but in the wood the air was cooler and smelled agreeably damp. Winnie had been no more than two slow minutes walking timidly under the interlacing branches when she wondered why she had never come here before. "Why, it's nice!" she thought with great surprise.

For the wood was full of light, entirely different from the light she was used to. It was green and amber and alive, quivering in splotches on the padded ground, fanning into sturdy stripes between the tree trunks. There were little flowers she did not recognize, white and palest blue; and endless, tangled vines; and here and there a fallen log, half rotted but soft with patches of sweet green-velvet moss.

And there were creatures everywhere. The air fairly hummed with their daybreak activity: beetles and birds and squirrels and ants, and countless other things unseen, all gentle and self-absorbed and not in the least alarming. There was even, she saw with satisfaction, the toad. It was squatting on a low stump and she might not have noticed it, for it looked more like a mushroom than a living creature sitting there. As she came abreast of it, however, it blinked, and the movement gave it away.

"See?" she exclaimed. "I told you I'd be here first thing in the morning."

The toad blinked again and nodded. Or perhaps it was only swallowing a fly. But then it nudged itself off the edge of the stump and vanished in the underbrush.

"It must have been watching for me," said Winnie to herself, and was very glad she had come.

She wandered for a long time, looking at everything, listening to everything, proud to forget the tight, pruned world outside, humming a little now, trying to remember the pattern of the melody she had heard the night before. And then, up ahead, in a place where the light seemed brighter and the ground somewhat more open, something moved.

Winnie stopped abruptly and crouched down. "If it's really elves," she thought, "I can have a look at them." And, though her instinct was to turn and run, she was pleased to discover that her curiosity was stronger. She began to creep forward. She would go just close enough, she told herself. Just close enough to see. And *then* she would turn and run. But when she came near, up behind a sheltering tree trunk, and peered around it, her mouth dropped open and all thought of running melted away.

There was a clearing directly in front of her, at the center of which an enormous tree thrust up, its thick roots rumpling the ground ten feet around in every direction. Sitting relaxed with his back against the trunk was a boy, almost a man. And he seemed so glorious to Winnie that she lost her heart at once.

He was thin and sunburned, this wonderful boy, with a thick mop of curly brown hair, and he wore his battered trousers and loose, grubby shirt with as much self-assurance as if they were silk and satin. A pair of green suspenders, more decorative than useful, gave the finishing touch, for he was shoeless and there was a twig tucked between the toes of one foot. He waved the twig idly as he sat there, his face turned up to gaze at the branches far above him. The golden morning light seemed to glow all around him, while brighter patches fell, now on his lean, brown hands, now on his hair and face, as the leaves stirred over his head.

Then he rubbed an ear carelessly, yawned, and stretched. Shifting his position, he turned his attention to a little pile of pebbles next to him. As Winnie watched, scarcely breathing, he moved the pile carefully to one side, pebble by pebble. Beneath the pile, the ground was shiny wet. The boy lifted a final stone and Winnie saw a low spurt of water, arching up and returning, like a fountain, into the ground. He bent and put his lips to the spurt, drinking noiselessly, and then he sat up again and drew his shirt sleeve across his mouth. As he did this, he turned his face in her direction—and their eyes met.

For a long moment they looked at each other in silence, the boy with his arm still raised to his mouth. Neither of them moved. At last his arm fell to his side. "You may as well come out," he said, with a frown.

Winnie stood up, embarrassed and, because of that, resentful. "I didn't mean to watch you," she protested as she stepped into the clearing. "I didn't know anyone would be here."

The boy eyed her as she came forward. "What're *you* doing here?" he asked her sternly.

"It's my wood," said Winnie, surprised by the question. "I can come here whenever I want to. At least, I was never here before, but I *could* have come, any time."

"Oh," said the boy, relaxing a little. "You're one of the Fosters, then."

"I'm Winnie," she said. "Who are you?"

"I'm Jesse Tuck," he answered. "How do." And he put out a hand.

Winnie took his hand, staring at him. He was even more beautiful up close. "Do you live nearby?" she managed at last, letting go of his hand reluctantly. "I never saw you before. Do you come here a lot? No one's supposed to. It's our wood." Then she added quickly, "It's all right, though, if *you* come here. I mean, it's all right with *me*."

The boy grinned. "No, I don't live nearby, and no, I don't come here often. Just passing through. And thanks, I'm glad it's all right with you."

"That's good," said Winnie irrelevantly. She stepped back and sat down primly a short distance from him. "How old are you, anyway?" she asked, squinting at him.

There was a pause. At last he said, "Why do you want to know?"

"I just wondered," said Winnie.

"All right. I'm one hundred and four years old," he told her solemnly.

"No, I mean really," she persisted.

"Well then," he said, "if you must know, I'm seventeen."

"Seventeen?"

"That's right."

"Oh," said Winnie hopelessly. "Seventeen. That's old."

"You have no idea," he agreed with a nod.

Winnie had the feeling he was laughing at her, but decided it was a nice kind of laughing. "Are you married?" she asked next.

This time he laughed out loud. "No, I'm not married. Are you?"

Now it was Winnie's turn to laugh. "Of course not," she said. "I'm only ten. But I'll be eleven pretty soon."

"And *then* you'll get married," he suggested.

Winnie laughed again, her head on one side, admiring him. And then she pointed to the spurt of water. "Is that good to drink?" she asked. "I'm thirsty."

Jesse Tuck's face was instantly serious. "Oh, that. No—no, it's not," he said quickly. "You mustn't drink from it. Comes right up out of the ground. Probably pretty dirty." And he began to pile the pebbles over it again.

"But *you* drank some," Winnie reminded him.

"Oh. Did you see that?" He looked at her anxiously. "Well, me, I'll drink anything. I mean, I'm used to it. It wouldn't be good for *you*, though."

"Why not?" said Winnie. She stood up. "It's mine, anyway, if it's in the wood. I want some. I'm about dry as dust." And she went to where he sat, and knelt down beside the pile of pebbles.

"Believe me, Winnie Foster," said Jesse, "it would be terrible for you if you drank any of this water. Just terrible. I can't let you."

"Well, I still don't see why not," said Winnie plaintively. "I'm getting thirstier every minute. If it didn't hurt you, it won't hurt me. If my papa was here, he'd let me have some."

"You're not going to tell him about it, are you?" said Jesse. His face had gone very pale under its sunburn. He stood up and put a bare foot firmly on the pile of pebbles. "I knew this would happen sooner or later. *Now* what am I going to do?"

As he said this, there was a crashing sound among the trees and a voice called, "Jesse?"

"Thank goodness!" said Jesse, blowing out his cheeks in relief. "Here comes Ma and Miles. They'll know what to do."

And sure enough, a big, comfortable-looking woman appeared, leading a fat old horse, and at her side was a young man almost as beautiful as Jesse. It was Mae Tuck with her other son, Jesse's older brother. And at once, when she saw the two of them, Jesse with his foot on the pile of pebbles and Winnie on her knees beside him, she seemed to understand. Her hand flew to her bosom, grasping at the old brooch that fastened her shawl, and her face went bleak. "Well, boys," she said, "here it is. The worst is happening at last."

6

Afterward, when she thought about it, it seemed to Winnie that the next few minutes were only a blur. First she was kneeling on the ground, insisting on a drink from the spring, and the next thing she knew, she was seized and swung through the air, open-mouthed, and found herself straddling the bouncing back of the fat old horse, with Miles and Jesse trotting along on either side, while Mae ran puffing ahead, dragging on the bridle.

Winnie had often been haunted by visions of what it would be like to be kidnapped. But none of her visions had been like this, with her kidnappers just as alarmed as she was herself. She had always pictured a troupe of burly men with long black moustaches who would tumble her into a blanket and bear her off like a sack of potatoes while she pleaded for mercy. But, instead, it was *they,* Mae Tuck and Miles and Jesse, who were pleading.

"Please, child . . . dear, dear child . . . don't you be scared." This was Mae, trying to run and call back over her shoulder at the same time. "We . . . wouldn't harm you . . . for the world."

"If you'd . . . yelled or anything"—this was Jesse —"someone might've heard you and . . . that's too risky."

And Miles said, "We'll explain it . . . soon as we're far enough away."

Winnie herself was speechless. She clung to the saddle and gave herself up to the astonishing fact that, though her heart was pounding and her backbone felt like a pipe full of cold running water, her head was fiercely calm. Disconnected thoughts presented themselves one by one, as if they had been waiting their turn in line. "So this is what it's like to ride a horse—I was going to run away today anyway—what will they say when I'm not there for breakfast—I wish the toad could see me now—that woman is worried about me—Miles is taller than Jesse—I'd better duck if I don't want this next branch to knock me off."

They had come to the edge of the wood now, with no sign of slowing their rapid jog. The road, where it angled across the meadow, was just ahead, dazzling white in the open sunlight. And there, standing on the road, was the man from the night before, the man in the yellow suit, his black hat on his head.

Discovering him, seeing his surprise, and presented at once with choices, Winnie's mind perversely went blank. Instead of crying out for help, she merely goggled at him as they fled past the spot where he stood. Mae Tuck was the only one who spoke, and the most she could offer was: "Teaching our little girl . . . how to ride!" Only then did it come to Winnie that she ought to shout, wave her arms, do *something*. But the man had fallen away behind by that time, and she was afraid to let go of the saddle, afraid to turn around, lest she fall off the horse. In another moment it was too late. They had sped up the hill and down its other side, and the opportunity was lost.

After another few minutes, the road led them to a place where, off to the left, a shallow stream looped near, with willows and sheltering, scrubby bushes. "Stop!" cried Mae. "We'll stop here!" Miles and Jesse grabbed at the horse's harness and he pulled up abruptly, nearly toppling Winnie off over his neck. "Lift the poor child down," Mae gasped, her chest heaving. "We'll go catch our breath by the water and try to put things straight before we go on."

But the explanation, once they had stumbled to the banks of the stream, came hard. Mae seemed embarrassed, and Miles and Jesse fidgeted, glancing at their mother uneasily. No one knew how to begin. For her part, Winnie, now that the running was over, began to comprehend what was happening, and with the comprehension her throat closed and her mouth went dry as paper. This was no vision. This was real. Strangers were taking her away; they might do anything; she might never see her mother again. And then, thinking of her mother, she saw herself as small, weak, and helpless, and she began to cry, suddenly, crushed as much by outrage as by shock.

Mae Tuck's round face wrinkled in dismay. "Dear Lord, don't cry! Please don't cry, child!" she implored. "We're not bad people, truly we're not. We *had* to bring you away—you'll see why in a minute —and we'll take you back just as soon as we can. Tomorrow. I promise."

When Mae said, "Tomorrow," Winnie's sobs turned to wails. Tomorrow! It was like being told she would be kept away forever. She wanted to go home now, at once, rush back to the safety of the fence and her mother's voice from the window. Mae reached out to her, but she twisted away, her hands over her face, and gave herself up to weeping.

"This is awful!" said Jesse. "Can't you do something, Ma? The poor little tad."

"We ought to've had some better plan than *this*," said Miles.

"That's the truth," said Mae helplessly. "The dear Lord knows there's been time enough to think of one, and it had to happen sooner or later. We been plain bone lucky it hasn't before now. But I never expected it'd be a *child!*" She reached distractedly into the pocket of her skirt and took out the music box and, without thinking, twisted the winding key with trembling fingers.

When the tinkling little melody began, Winnie's sobbing slowed. She stood by the stream, her hands still over her face, and listened. Yes, it was the same music she had heard the night before. Somehow it calmed her. It was like a ribbon tying her to familiar things. She thought, "When I get home, I'll tell Granny it wasn't elf music after all." She wiped her face as well as she could with her wet hands and turned to Mae. "That's the music I heard last night," she managed between recovering snuffles. "When I was out in my yard. My granny said it was elves."

"Dear me, no," said Mae, peering at her hopefully. "It's only my music box. I didn't suppose anyone could hear it." She held it out to Winnie. "Do you want to take a look at it?"

"It's pretty," said Winnie, taking the little box and turning it over in her hands. The winding key was still revolving, but more and more slowly. The melody faltered. Another few widely spaced notes plinked, and then it stopped.

"Wind it up if you want to," said Mae. "Clockwise."

Winnie turned the key. It clicked faintly. And then, after several more turns, the music began to play again, brisk from its fresh winding, and merry. No one who owned a thing like this could be too disagreeable. Winnie examined the painted roses and lilies of the valley, and smiled in spite of herself. "It's pretty," she repeated, handing it back to Mae.

The music box had relaxed them all. Miles dragged a handkerchief from a back pocket and mopped at his face, and Mae sank down heavily on a rock, pulling off the blue straw hat and fanning herself with it.

"Look here, Winnie Foster," said Jesse. "We're friends, we really are. But you got to help us. Come sit down, and we'll try to tell you why."

7

It was the strangest story Winnie had ever heard. She soon suspected they had never told it before, except to each other—that she was their first real audience; for they gathered around her like children at their mother's knee, each trying to claim her attention, and sometimes they all talked at once, and interrupted each other, in their eagerness.

Eighty-seven years before, the Tucks had come from a long way to the east, looking for a place to settle. In those days the wood was not a wood, it was a forest, just as her grandmother had said: a forest that went on and on and on. They had thought they would start a farm, as soon as they came to the end of the trees. But the trees never seemed to end. When they came to the part that was now the wood, and turned from the trail to find a camping place, they happened on the spring. "It was real nice," said Jesse with a sigh. "It looked just the way it does now. A clearing, lots of sunshine, that big tree with all those knobby roots. We stopped and everyone took a drink, even the horse."

"No," said Mae, "the cat didn't drink. That's important."

"Yes," said Miles, "don't leave that out. We all had a drink, except for the cat."

"Well, anyway," Jesse went on, "the water tasted —sort of strange. But we camped there overnight. And Pa carved a T on the tree trunk, to mark where we'd been. And then we went on."

They had come out of the forest at last, many miles to the west, had found a thinly populated valley, had started their farm. "We put up a house for Ma and Pa," said Miles, "and a little shack for Jesse and me. We figured *we'd* be starting families of our own pretty soon and would want our own houses."

"That was the first time we figured there was something peculiar," said Mae. "Jesse fell out of a tree . . ."

"I was way up in the middle," Jesse interrupted, "trying to saw off some of the big branches before we cut her down. I lost my balance and I fell . . ."

"He landed plum on his head," said Mae with a shudder. "We thought for sure he'd broke his neck. But come to find out, it didn't hurt him a bit!"

"Not long after," Miles went on, "some hunters

come by one day at sunset. The horse was out grazing by some trees and they shot him. Mistook him for a deer, they said. Can you fancy that? But the thing is, they didn't kill him. The bullet went right on through him, and didn't hardly even leave a mark."

"Then Pa got snake bite . . ."

"And Jesse ate the poison toadstools . . ."

"And I cut myself," said Mae. "Remember? Slicing bread."

But it was the passage of time that worried them most. They had worked the farm, settled down, made friends. But after ten years, then twenty, they had to face the fact that there was something terribly wrong. None of them was getting any older.

"I was more'n forty by then," said Miles sadly. "I was married. I had two children. But, from the look of me, I was still twenty-two. My wife, she finally made up her mind I'd sold my soul to the Devil. She left me. She went away and she took the children with her."

"I'm glad *I* never got married," Jesse put in.

"It was the same with our friends," said Mae. "They come to pull back from us. There was talk about witchcraft. Black magic. Well, you can't hardly blame them, but finally we had to leave the farm. We didn't know where to go. We started back the way we come, just wandering. We was like gypsies. When we got this far, it'd changed, of course. A lot

of the trees was gone. There was people, and Treegap
—it was a new village. The road was here, but in
those days it was mostly just a cow path. We went on
into what was left of the wood to make a camp, and
when we got to the clearing and the tree and the
spring, we remembered it from before."

"*It* hadn't changed, no more'n we had," said Miles.
"And that was how we found out. Pa'd carved a T on
the tree, remember, twenty years before, but the T
was just where it'd been when he done it. That tree
hadn't grown one whit in all that time. It was exactly the same. And the T he'd carved was as fresh
as if it'd just been put there."

Then they had remembered drinking the water.
They—and the horse. But not the cat. The cat had
lived a long and happy life on the farm, but had died
some ten years before. So they decided at last that
the source of their changelessness was the spring.

"When we come to that conclusion," Mae went
on, "Tuck said—that's my husband, Angus Tuck—
he said he had to be sure, once and for all. He took
his shotgun and he pointed it at hisself the best way
he could, and before we could stop him, he pulled
the trigger." There was a long pause. Mae's fingers,
laced together in her lap, twisted with the tension of
remembering. At last she said, "The shot knocked
him down. Went into his heart. It *had* to, the way
he aimed. And right on through him. It scarcely even

left a mark. Just like—*you* know—like you shot a bullet through water. And he was just the same as if he'd never done it."

"After that we went sort of crazy," said Jesse, grinning at the memory. "Heck, we was going to live forever. Can you picture what it felt like to find that out?"

"But then we sat down and talked it over . . ." said Miles.

"We're still talking it over," Jesse added.

"And we figured it'd be very bad if everyone knowed about that spring," said Mae. "We begun to see what it would mean." She peered at Winnie. "Do you understand, child? That water—it stops you right where you are. If you'd had a drink of it today, you'd stay a little girl forever. You'd never grow up, not ever."

"We don't know how it works, or even why," said Miles.

"Pa thinks it's something left over from—well, from some other plan for the way the world should be," said Jesse. "Some plan that didn't work out too good. And so everything was changed. Except that the spring was passed over, somehow or other. Maybe he's right. *I* don't know. But you see, Winnie Foster, when I told you before I'm a hundred and four years old, I was telling the truth. But I'm really only seventeen. And, so far as I know, I'll stay seventeen till the end of the world."

8

Winnie did not believe in fairy tales. She had never longed for a magic wand, did not expect to marry a prince, and was scornful—most of the time—of her grandmother's elves. So now she sat, mouth open, wide-eyed, not knowing what to make of this extraordinary story. It couldn't—not a bit of it—be true. And yet:

"It feels so fine to tell somebody!" Jesse exploded. "Just think, Winnie Foster, you're the only person in the world, besides us, who knows about it!"

"Hold on now," said Miles cautiously. "Maybe not. There might be a whole lot of others, for all we know, wandering around just like us."

"Maybe. But *we* don't know them," Jesse pointed out. "We've never had anyone but us to talk about it to. Winnie—isn't it peculiar? And kind of wonderful? Just think of all the things we've seen in the world! All the things we're going to see!"

"That kind of talk'll make her want to rush back and drink a gallon of the stuff," warned Miles. "There's a whole lot more to it than Jesse Tuck's good times, you know."

"Oh, stuff," said Jesse with a shrug. "We might as well enjoy it, long as we can't change it. You don't have to be such a parson all the time."

"I'm not being a parson," said Miles. "I just think you ought to take it more serious."

"Now, boys," said Mae. She was kneeling by the stream, splashing her face and hands with cool water. "Whew! Such weather!" she exclaimed, sitting back on her heels. She unfastened the brooch, took off her shawl, and toweled her dripping face. "Well, child," she said to Winnie, standing up, "now you share our secret. It's a big, dangerous secret. We got to have your help to keep it. I expect you're full of questions, but we can't stay here no longer." She tied the shawl around her waist then, and sighed. "It pains me to think how your ma and pa will worry, but there's just no way around it. We got to take you home with us. That's the plan. Tuck—he'll want to talk it out, make sure you see why you can't tell no one. But we'll bring you back tomorrow. All right?" And all three of them looked at her hopefully.

"All right," said Winnie. For, she decided, there

wasn't any choice. She would have to go. They would probably make her go, anyway, no matter what she said. But she felt there was nothing to be afraid of, not really. For they seemed gentle. Gentle and—in a strange way—childlike. They made her feel old. And the way they spoke to her, the way they looked at her, made her feel special. Important. It was a warm, spreading feeling, entirely new. She liked it, and in spite of their story, she liked them, too—especially Jesse.

But it was Miles who took her hand and said, "It's really fine to have you along, even if it's only for a day or two."

Then Jesse gave a great whoop and leapt into the stream, splashing mightily. "What'd you bring for breakfast, Ma?" he cried. "We can eat on the way, can't we? I'm starving!"

So, with the sun riding high now in the sky, they started off again, noisy in the August stillness, eating bread and cheese. Jesse sang funny old songs in a loud voice and swung like a monkey from the branches of trees, showing off shamelessly for Winnie, calling to her, "Hey, Winnie Foster, watch me!" and "Look what I can do!"

And Winnie, laughing at him, lost the last of her alarm. They were friends, *her* friends. She was running away after all, but she was not alone. Closing the gate on her oldest fears as she had closed the gate of her own fenced yard, she discovered the wings she'd always wished she had. And all at once she was elated. Where were the terrors she'd been told she should expect? She could not recognize them anywhere. The sweet earth opened out its wide four corners to her like the petals of a flower ready to be picked, and it shimmered with light and possibility till she was dizzy with it. Her mother's voice, the feel of home, receded for the moment, and her thoughts turned forward. Why, she, too, might live forever in this remarkable world she was only just discovering! The story of the spring—it might be true! So that, when she was not rolling along on the back of the fat old horse—by choice, this time—she ran shouting down the road, her arms flung out, making more noise than anybody.

It was good. So good, in fact, that through it all, not one of them noticed that the man they had passed on the road, the man in the yellow suit, had crept up to the bushes by the stream and heard it all, the whole fantastic story. Nor did they notice that he was following now, beside the road far behind, his mouth, above the thin, gray beard, turned ever so slightly toward a smile.

9

The August sun rolled up, hung at mid-heaven for a blinding hour, and at last wheeled westward before the journey was done. But Winnie was exhausted long before that. Miles carried her some of the way. The tops of her cheeks were bright pink with sunburn, her nose a vivid, comic red, but she had been rescued from a more serious broiling by Mae, who had finally insisted that she wear the blue straw hat. It came down far over her ears and gave her a clownish appearance, but the shade from its brim was so welcome that Winnie put vanity aside and dozed gratefully in Miles's strong arms, her own arms wound around his neck.

The pastures, fields, and scrubby groves they crossed were vigorous with bees, and crickets leapt before them as if each step released a spring and flung them up like pebbles. But everything else was motionless, dry as biscuit, on the brink of burning, hoarding final reservoirs of sap, trying to hold out till the rain returned, and Queen Anne's lace lay dusty on the surface of the meadows like foam on a painted sea.

It was amazing, then, to climb a long hill, to see ahead another hill, and beyond that the deep green of a scattered pine forest, and as you climbed, to feel the air ease and soften. Winnie revived, sniffing, and was able to ride the horse again, perched behind Mae. And to her oft-repeated question, "Are we almost there?" the welcome answer came at last: "Only a few more minutes now."

A wide stand of dark pines rose up, loomed nearer, and suddenly Jesse was crying, "We're home! This is it, Winnie Foster!" And he and Miles raced on and disappeared among the trees. The horse followed, turning onto a rutted path lumpy with roots, and it was as if they had slipped in under a giant colander. The late sun's brilliance could penetrate only in scattered glimmers, and everything was silent and untouched, the ground muffled with moss and sliding needles, the graceful arms of the pines stretched out protectively in every direction. And it was cool, blessedly cool and green. The horse picked his way carefully, and then ahead the path dropped down a steep embankment; and beyond that, Winnie, peering around Mae's bulk, saw a flash of color and a dazzling sparkle. Down the embankment they swayed and there it was, a plain, homely little house, barn-red, and below it the last of the sun flashing on the wrinkled surface of a tiny lake.

"Oh, *look!*" cried Winnie. "Water!"

At the same time, they heard two enormous splashes, two voices roaring with pleasure.

"It don't take 'em more'n a minute to pile into that pond," said Mae, beaming. "Well, you can't blame 'em in heat like this. You can go in, too, if you want."

Then they were at the door of the little house and Tuck was standing there. "Where's the child?" he demanded, for Winnie was hidden behind his wife. "The boys say you brung along a real, honest-to-goodness, natural child!"

"So I did," said Mae, sliding down off the horse, "and here she is."

Winnie's shyness returned at once when she saw the big man with his sad face and baggy trousers, but as he gazed at her, the warm, pleasing feeling spread through her again. For Tuck's head tilted to one side, his eyes went soft, and the gentlest smile in the world displaced the melancholy creases of his cheeks. He reached up to lift her from the horse's back and he said, "There's just no words to tell you how happy I am to see you. It's the finest thing that's happened in . . ." He interrupted himself, setting Winnie on the ground, and turned to Mae. "Does she know?"

"Course she knows," said Mae. "That's why I brung her back. Winnie, here's my husband, Angus Tuck. Tuck, meet Winnie Foster."

"How do, Winnie Foster," said Tuck, shaking Winnie's hand rather solemnly. "Well, then!" He straightened and peered down at her, and Winnie, looking back into his face, saw an expression there that made her feel like an unexpected present, wrapped in pretty paper and tied with ribbons, in spite of Mae's blue hat, which still enveloped her head. "Well, then," Tuck repeated, "seeing you know, I'll go on and say this is the finest thing that's happened in—oh—at least eighty years."

10

Winnie had grown up with order. She was used to it. Under the pitiless double assaults of her mother and grandmother, the cottage where she lived was always squeaking clean, mopped and swept and scoured into limp submission. There was no room for carelessness, no putting things off until later. The Foster women had made a fortress out of duty. Within it, they were indomitable. And Winnie was in training.

So she was unprepared for the homely little house beside the pond, unprepared for the gentle eddies of dust, the silver cobwebs, the mouse who lived—and welcome to him!—in a table drawer. There were only three rooms. The kitchen came first, with an open cabinet where dishes were stacked in perilous towers without the least regard for their varying dimensions. There was an enormous black stove, and a metal sink, and every surface, every wall, was piled and strewn and hung with everything imaginable, from onions to lanterns to wooden spoons to wash-tubs. And in a corner stood Tuck's forgotten shot-gun.

The parlor came next, where the furniture, loose and sloping with age, was set about helter-skelter. An ancient green-plush sofa lolled alone in the center, like yet another mossy fallen log, facing a soot-streaked fireplace still deep in last winter's ashes. The table with the drawer that housed the mouse was pushed off, also alone, into a far corner, and three armchairs and an elderly rocker stood about aimlessly, like strangers at a party, ignoring each other.

Beyond this was the bedroom, where a vast and tipsy brass bed took up most of the space, but there was room beside it for the washstand with the lonely mirror, and opposite its foot a cavernous oak ward-robe from which leaked the faint smell of camphor.

Up a steep flight of narrow stairs was a dusty loft —"That's where the boys sleep when they're home," Mae explained—and that was all. And yet it was not quite all. For there was everywhere evidence of their activities, Mae's and Tuck's. Her sewing: patches and scraps of bright cloth; half-completed quilts and braided rugs; a bag of cotton batting with wisps of its contents, like snow, drifting into cracks and corners; the arms of the sofa webbed with strands of thread and dangerous with needles. His wood carving: curly shavings furring the floor, and little heaps of splinters and chips; every surface dim with the sawdust of countless sandings; limbs of unassembled dolls and wooden soldiers; a ship model propped on the mouse's table, waiting for its glue to dry; and a stack of wooden bowls, their sides smoothed to velvet, the topmost bowl filled with a jumble of big wooden spoons and forks, like dry, bleached bones. "We make things to sell," said Mae, surveying the mess approvingly.

And still this was not all. For, on the old beamed ceiling of the parlor, streaks of light swam and danced and wavered like a bright mirage, reflected through the windows from the sunlit surface of the pond. There were bowls of daisies everywhere, gay white and yellow. And over everything was the clean, sweet smell of the water and its weeds, the chatter of a swooping kingfisher, the carol and trill of a dozen other kinds of bird, and occasionally the thrilling bass note of an unastonished bullfrog at ease somewhere along the muddy banks.

Into it all came Winnie, eyes wide, and very much amazed. It was a whole new idea to her that people could live in such disarray, but at the same time she was charmed. It was . . . comfortable. Climbing behind Mae up the stairs to see the loft, she thought to herself: "Maybe it's because they think they have forever to clean it up." And this was followed by another thought, far more revolutionary: "Maybe they just don't care!"

"The boys don't be home very much," said Mae as they came up into the half light of the loft. "But when they are, they bed up here. There's plenty of room." The loft was cluttered, too, with all kinds of odds and ends, but there were two mattresses rolled out on the floor, and fresh sheets and blankets were folded almost neatly on each, waiting to be spread.

"Where do they go when they're away?" asked Winnie. "What do they do?"

"Oh," said Mae, "they go different places, do different things. They work at what jobs they can get, try to bring home some of their money. Miles can do carpentering, and he's a pretty fair blacksmith, too. Jesse now, *he* don't ever seem too settled in himself. Course, he's young." She stopped and smiled. "That sounds funny, don't it? Still, it's true, just the same. So Jesse, he does what strikes him at the moment, working in the fields, or in saloons, things like that, whatever he comes across. But they can't stay on in any one place for long, you know. None of us can. People get to wondering." She sighed. "We been in this house about as long as we dare, going on twenty years. It's a right nice place. Tuck's got so's he's real attached to it. Then, too, it's off by itself, plenty of fish in the pond, not too far from the towns around. When we need things, we go sometimes to one, sometimes the next, so people don't come to notice us much. And we sell where we can. But I guess we'll be moving on, one of these days. It's just about time."

It sounded rather sad to Winnie, never to belong anywhere. "That's too bad," she said, glancing shyly at Mae. "Always moving around and never having any friends or anything."

But Mae shrugged off this observation. "Tuck and me, we got each other," she said, "and that's a lot. The boys, now, they go their separate ways. They're some different, don't always get on too good. But they come home whenever the spirit moves, and every ten years, first week of August, they meet at the spring and come home *together* so's we can be a family again for a little while. That's why we was there this morning. One way or another, it all works out." She folded her arms and nodded, more to herself than to Winnie. "Life's got to be lived, no matter how long or short," she said calmly. "You got to take what comes. We just go along, like everybody else, one day at a time. Funny—we don't feel no different. Leastways, I don't. Sometimes I forget about what's happened to us, forget it altogether. And then sometimes it comes over me and I wonder why it happened to *us*. We're plain as salt, us Tucks. We don't deserve no blessings—if it is a blessing. And, likewise, I don't see how we deserve to be cursed, if it's a curse. Still—there's no use trying to figure why things fall the way they do. Things just are, and fussing don't bring changes. Tuck, now, he's got a few other ideas, but I expect he'll tell you. There! The boys are in from the pond."

Winnie heard a burst of voices downstairs, and in a moment Miles and Jesse were climbing to the loft.

"Here, child," said Mae hastily. "Hide your eyes. Boys? Are you decent? What'd you put on to swim in? I got Winnie up here, do you hear me?"

"For goodness' sake, Ma," said Jesse, emerging from the stairwell. "You think we're going to march around in our altogether with Winnie Foster in the house?"

And Miles, behind him, said, "We just jumped in with our clothes on. Too hot and tired to shed 'em."

It was true. They stood there side by side with their wet clothes plastered to their skins, little pools of water collecting at their feet.

"Well!" said Mae, relieved. "All right. Find something dry to put on. Your pa's got supper nearly ready." And she hustled Winnie down the narrow stairs.

11

It was a good supper, flapjacks, bacon, bread, and applesauce, but they ate sitting about in the parlor instead of around a table. Winnie had never had a meal that way before and she watched them carefully at first, to see what rules there might be that she did not know about. But there seemed to be no rules. Jesse sat on the floor and used the seat of a chair for a table, but the others held their plates in their laps. There were no napkins. It was all right, then, to lick the maple syrup from your fingers. Winnie was never allowed to do such a thing at home, but she had always thought it would be the easiest way. And suddenly the meal seemed luxurious.

After a few minutes, however, it was clear to Winnie that there was at least one rule: As long as there was food to eat, there was no conversation. All four

Tucks kept their eyes and their attention on the business at hand. And in the silence, given time to think, Winnie felt her elation, and her thoughtless pleasure, wobble and collapse.

It had been different when they were out-of-doors, where the world belonged to everyone and no one. Here, everything was theirs alone, everything was done their way. Eating, she realized now, was a very personal thing, not something to do with strangers. *Chewing* was a personal thing. Yet here she was, chewing with strangers in a strange place. She shivered a little, and frowned, looking round at them. That story they had told her—why, they were crazy, she thought harshly, and they were criminals. They had kidnapped her, right out of the middle of her very own wood, and now she would be expected to sleep —*all night*—in this dirty, peculiar house. She had never slept in any bed but her own in her life. All these thoughts flowed at once from the dark part of her mind. She put down her fork and said, unsteadily, "I want to go home."

The Tucks stopped eating, and looked at her, surprised. Mae said soothingly, "Why, of course you do, child. That's only natural. I'll take you home. I promised I would, soon's we've explained a bit as to why you got to promise you'll never tell about the spring. That's the only reason we brung you here. We got to make you see why."

Then Miles said, cheerfully and with sudden sympathy, "There's a pretty good old rowboat. I'll take you out for a row after supper."

"No, *I* will," said Jesse. "Let *me*. I found her first, didn't I, Winnie Foster? Listen, I'll show you where the frogs are, and . . ."

"Hush," Tuck interrupted. "Everyone hush. *I'll* take Winnie rowing on the pond. There's a good deal to be said and I think we better hurry up and say it. I got a feeling there ain't a whole lot of time."

Jesse laughed at this, and ran a hand roughly through his curls. "That's funny, Pa. Seems to me like time's the only thing we got a lot of."

But Mae frowned. "You worried, Tuck? What's got you? No one saw us on the way up. Well, now, wait a bit—yes, they did, come to think of it. There was a man on the road, just outside Treegap. But he didn't say nothing."

"He knows me, though," said Winnie. She had forgotten, too, about the man in the yellow suit, and now, thinking of him, she felt a surge of relief. "He'll tell my father he saw me."

"He knows you?" said Mae, her frown deepening. "But you didn't call out to him, child. Why not?"

"I was too scared to do *anything*," said Winnie honestly.

Tuck shook his head. "I never thought we'd come to the place where we'd be scaring children," he said. "I guess there's no way to make it up to you, Winnie, but I'm sure most awful sorry it had to happen like that. Who was this man you saw?"

"I don't know his name," said Winnie. "But he's a pretty nice man, I guess." In fact, he seemed supremely nice to her now, a kind of savior. And then she added, "He came to our house last night, but he didn't go inside."

"Well, that don't sound too serious, Pa," said Miles. "Just some stranger passing by."

"Just the same, we got to get you home again, Winnie," said Tuck, standing up decisively. "We got to get you home just as fast as we can. I got a feeling this whole thing is going to come apart like wet bread. But first we got to talk, and the pond's the best place. The pond's got answers. Come along, child. Let's go out on the water."

12

The sky was a ragged blaze of red and pink and orange, and its double trembled on the surface of the pond like color spilled from a paintbox. The sun was dropping fast now, a soft red sliding egg yolk, and already to the east there was a darkening to purple. Winnie, newly brave with her thoughts of being rescued, climbed boldly into the rowboat. The hard heels of her buttoned boots made a hollow banging sound against its wet boards, loud in the warm and breathless quiet. Across the pond a bullfrog spoke a deep note of warning. Tuck climbed in, too, pushing off, and, settling the oars into their locks, dipped them into the silty bottom in one strong pull. The rowboat slipped from the bank then, silently, and glided out, tall water grasses whispering away from its sides, releasing it.

Here and there the still surface of the water dimpled, and bright rings spread noiselessly and vanished. "Feeding time," said Tuck softly. And Winnie, looking down, saw hosts of tiny insects skittering and skating on the surface. "Best time of all for fishing," he said, "when they come up to feed."

He dragged on the oars. The rowboat slowed and began to drift gently toward the farthest end of the pond. It was so quiet that Winnie almost jumped when the bullfrog spoke again. And then, from the tall pines and birches that ringed the pond, a wood thrush caroled. The silver notes were pure and clear and lovely.

"Know what that is, all around us, Winnie?" said Tuck, his voice low. "Life. Moving, growing, changing, never the same two minutes together. This water, you look out at it every morning, and it *looks* the same, but it ain't. All night long it's been moving, coming in through the stream back there to the west, slipping out through the stream down east here, always quiet, always new, moving on. You can't hardly see the current, can you? And sometimes the wind makes it look like it's going the other way. But it's always there, the water's always moving on, and someday, after a long while, it comes to the ocean."

They drifted in silence for a time. The bullfrog spoke again, and from behind them, far back in some reedy, secret place, another bullfrog answered. In the fading light, the trees along the banks were slowly losing their dimensions, flattening into silhouettes clipped from black paper and pasted to the paling sky. The voice of a different frog, hoarser and not so deep, croaked from the nearest bank.

"Know what happens then?" said Tuck. "To the water? The sun sucks some of it up right out of the ocean and carries it back in clouds, and then it rains, and the rain falls into the stream, and the stream keeps moving on, taking it all back again. It's a wheel, Winnie. Everything's a wheel, turning and turning, never stopping. The frogs is part of it, and the bugs, and the fish, and the wood thrush, too. And people. But never the same ones. Always coming in new, always growing and changing, and always moving on. That's the way it's supposed to be. That's the way it *is*."

The rowboat had drifted at last to the end of the pond, but now its bow bumped into the rotting branches of a fallen tree that thrust thick fingers into the water. And though the current pulled at it, dragging its stern sidewise, the boat was wedged and could not follow. The water slipped past it, out between clumps of reeds and brambles, and gurgled down a narrow bed, over stones and pebbles, foaming a little, moving swiftly now after its slow trip between the pond's wide banks. And, farther down,

Winnie could see that it hurried into a curve, around a leaning willow, and disappeared.

"It goes on," Tuck repeated, "to the ocean. But this rowboat now, it's stuck. If we didn't move it out ourself, it would stay here forever, trying to get loose, but stuck. That's what us Tucks are, Winnie. Stuck so's we can't move on. We ain't part of the wheel no more. Dropped off, Winnie. Left behind. And everywhere around us, things is moving and growing and changing. You, for instance. A child now, but someday a woman. And after that, moving on to make room for the new children."

Winnie blinked, and all at once her mind was drowned with understanding of what he was saying. For she—yes, even she—would go out of the world willy-nilly someday. Just go out, like the flame of a candle, and no use protesting. It was a certainty. She would try very hard not to think of it, but sometimes, as now, it would be forced upon her. She raged against it, helpless and insulted, and blurted at last, "I don't want to die."

"No," said Tuck calmly. "Not now. Your time's not now. But dying's part of the wheel, right there next to being born. You can't pick out the pieces you like and leave the rest. Being part of the whole thing, that's the blessing. But it's passing us by, us Tucks. Living's heavy work, but off to one side, the way *we* are, it's useless, too. It don't make sense. If I knowed how to climb back on the wheel, I'd do it in a minute. You can't have living without dying. So you can't call it living, what we got. We just *are,* we just *be,* like rocks beside the road."

Tuck's voice was rough now, and Winnie, amazed, sat rigid. No one had ever talked to her of things like this before. "I want to grow again," he said fiercely, "and change. And if that means I got to move on at the end of it, then I want that, too. Listen, Winnie, it's something you don't find out how you feel until afterwards. If people knowed about the spring down there in Treegap, they'd all come running like pigs to slops. They'd trample each other, trying to get some of that water. That'd be bad enough, but after-wards—can you imagine? All the little ones little forever, all the old ones old forever. Can you picture what that means? *Forever?* The wheel would keep on going round, the water rolling by to the ocean, but the people would've turned into nothing but rocks by the side of the road. 'Cause they wouldn't know till after, and then it'd be too late." He peered at her, and Winnie saw that his face was pinched with the effort of explaining. "Do you see, now, child? Do you understand? Oh, Lord, I just got to make you understand!"

There was a long, long moment of silence. Winnie, struggling with the anguish of all these things, could only sit hunched and numb, the sound of the water rolling in her ears. It was black and silky now; it lapped at the sides of the rowboat and hurried on around them into the stream.

And then, down the length of the pond, a voice rang out. It was Miles, and every word, across the water, came clearly to their ears. "Pa! Pa, come back! Something's happened, Pa. The horse is gone. Can you hear me? Someone's stole the horse."

13

Sometime later, the man in the yellow suit slipped down from the saddle and tied the Tucks' old horse to a bar of the Fosters' fence. He tried the gate. It was unlocked. He pushed through and strode up the path to the door of the cottage. Though it was very late now, almost midnight, the windows glowed golden: the family had not gone to bed. The man in the yellow suit took off his hat and smoothed his hair with long white fingers. Then he knocked at the door. It was opened at once by Winnie's grandmother, and before she could speak, the man said quickly, "Ah! Good evening! May I come in? I have happy news for you. I know where they've taken the little girl."

14

There had been nothing for the Tucks to do but go to bed. It was too dark now to go out looking for the horse thief, and anyway, they had no idea when he had done his thieving or which way he had gone.

"That beats all, though, don't it, Pa," said Jesse, "coming up to a person's house and stealing their horse right out from under their nose!"

"I got to give you that," said Tuck. "But the question is, was it just some ordinary thief, or was it someone that had some special reason? I don't like it. I got a bad feeling about the whole thing."

"Hush now, Tuck," said Mae. She was spreading a quilt on the old sofa, making it into a bed for Winnie. "You're too much of a worrier. There's nothing we can do about it now, so there's no sense fussing. You got no reason to think there's anything peculiar about it, anyway. Come on, we'll get a good night's sleep and figure it out in the morning when we're fresh. Boys, up you go, and don't get talking—you'll keep us awake. Winnie, child, you bed down, too. You'll sleep first-rate on the sofa here."

But Winnie did not sleep at all, not for a long, long time. The cushions of the sofa were remarkably lumpy and smelled like old newspapers; and the chair pad Mae had given her for a pillow was thin and hard, and rough under her cheek. But far worse than this was the fact that she was still in her clothes, for she had firmly refused the offer of Mae's spare nightgown, with its seeming miles of faded cotton flannel. Only her own nightgown would do, and the regular bedtime routine; without them, she was painfully lonely for home. Her joy on the road that morning had completely disappeared; the wide world shrank and her oldest fears rolled freely in her consciousness. It was unbelievable that she should be in this place; it was an outrage. But she was helpless to do anything about it, helpless to control it, and exhausted by the conversation in the rowboat.

Was it true? Could they really never die, these Tucks? It had evidently not occurred to them that she might not believe it. They were only concerned that she keep the secret. Well, she did not believe it. It was nonsense. Wasn't it? Well, wasn't it?

Winnie's head whirled. Remembering the man in

the yellow suit was the only thing that kept her from weeping. "He's told them by now," she thought, rehearsing it. "They've been looking for me for hours. But they don't know where to look! No. The man saw which way we were headed. Papa will find me. They're out looking for me right now."

She went over it again and again, lying wrapped in the quilt, while outside the moon rose, turning the pond to silver. There was a hint of mist, now that the air was cooler, and the frogs talked comfortably. Crickets soon joined in with their shrill, rhythmic song. In the table drawer, the mouse rustled softly, enjoying the supper of flapjack crumbs Mae had put there for him. And at last these things were clearer in Winnie's ears than the voice of her thoughts. She began to relax, listening to the sound-filled silence. Then, just as she was drifting into sleep, she heard soft footsteps and Mae was beside her. "You resting easy, child?" she whispered.

"I'm all right, thank you," said Winnie.

"I'm sorry about everything," said Mae. "I just didn't know no other way but to bring you back with us. I know it ain't very happy for you here, but ... well ... anyway, you have a good talk with Tuck?"

"I guess so," said Winnie.

"That's good. Well. I'm going back to bed. Get a good sleep."

"All right," said Winnie.

But still Mae lingered. "We been alone so long," she said at last, "I guess we don't know how to do with visitors. But still and all, it's a good feeling, you being here with us. I wish you was . . . ours." She put out an awkward hand then and touched Winnie's hair. "Well," she said, "good night."

"Good night," said Winnie.

Tuck came, too, a little later, to peer down at her anxiously. He was wearing a long white nightshirt and his hair was rumpled. "Oh!" he said. "You still awake? Everything all right?"

"Yes," said Winnie.

"I didn't mean to go disturbing you," he said. "But I been laying in there thinking I ought to be setting out here with you till you went to sleep."

"You don't have to do that," said Winnie, surprised and touched. "I'm all right."

He looked uncertain. "Well . . . but if you want something, will you holler? I'm just in the next room —I'd be out here like a shot." And then he added, gruffly, "It's been quite a time since we had a natural, growing child in the house . . ." His voice trailed off. "Well. Try to get some sleep. That sofa there, I guess it ain't the kind of thing you're used to."

"It's fine," said Winnie.

"The bed's no better, or I'd switch with you," he said. He didn't seem to know how to finish the conversation. But then he bent and kissed her quickly on the cheek, and was gone.

Winnie lay with her eyes wide. She felt cared for and—confused. And all at once she wondered what would happen to the Tucks when her father came. What would he do to them? She would never be able to explain how they had been with her, how they made her feel. She remembered guiltily that at supper she had decided they were criminals. Well, but they *were*. And yet . . .

And then a final visitor made her confusion complete. There was a creaking on the loft stairs and Jesse was looking down at her, very beautiful and eager in the faint blue moonlight. "Hey, Winnie Foster," he whispered. "You asleep?"

This time she sat up, pulling the quilt around her in sudden embarrassment, and answered, "No, not yet."

"Well then, listen." He knelt beside her, his curls tumbled and his eyes wide. "I been thinking it over. Pa's right about you having to keep the secret. It's not hard to see why. But the thing is, you knowing about the water already, and living right next to it so's you could go there any time, well, listen, how'd it be if you was to wait till you're seventeen, same age as me—heck, that's only six years off—and then you could go and drink some, and then you could go away with me! We could get married, even. That'd be pretty good, wouldn't it! We could have a grand old time, go all around the world, see everything. Listen, Ma and Pa and Miles, they don't know how to enjoy it, what we got. Why, heck, Winnie, life's to enjoy yourself, isn't it? What else is it good for? That's what *I* say. And you and me, we could have a good time that never, never stopped. Wouldn't that be something?"

Once more Winnie adored him, kneeling there beside her in the moonlight. He wasn't crazy. How could he be? He was just—amazing. But she was struck dumb. All she could do was stare at him.

"You think on it, Winnie Foster," Jesse whispered earnestly. "Think on it some and see if it don't sound good. Anyway, I'll see you in the morning. All right?"

"All right," she managed to whisper in return. He slipped away then, back up the creaking steps, but Winnie sat upright, wide awake, her cheeks burning. She could not deal with this remarkable suggestion, she could not "think on it." For she didn't know what to believe about anything. She lay down again, finally, and stared into the moonlight for another half an hour before she fell asleep.

15

In Treegap, the same moonlight silvered the roof of the touch-me-not cottage, but inside, the lamps were burning. "That's right," said the man in the yellow suit. "I know where she is." He sat back in his chair in the Fosters' spotless parlor, crossing his long, thin legs, and the suspended foot began a rhythmic jiggling. He hung his hat on his knee and smiled, his eyes nearly closed. "I followed them, you see. She's with them now. As soon as I saw they'd arrived at their destination, I turned around and came directly back. I thought you'd be staying up. You've been looking for her all day, of course. It must be quite a worry."

He lifted a hand then, ignoring their exclamations, and began to smooth the thin hairs of his beard. "You know," he said thoughtfully, "I've come a long way, looking for a wood exactly like the one you've got next door here. It would mean a great deal to me to own it. And how pleasant to have neighbors like yourselves! Now, understand, I wouldn't cut down many of the trees. I'm no barbarian, you can see that. No, just a few. You wouldn't find it different at all, really." He gestured with his long, white fingers and smiled, his face crinkling pleasantly. "We'd be good friends, I think. Why, the little girl and I, we're friends already. It would be a great relief to see her safely home again, wouldn't it?" He clicked his tongue and frowned. "Dreadful thing, kidnapping. Isn't it fortunate that I was a witness! Why, without me, you might never have heard a word. They're rough country people, the ones that took her. There's just no telling what illiterates like that might do. Yes," he sighed, lifting his eyebrows and smiling again, "it looks as if I'm the only person in the whole world who knows where to find her."

And then the man in the yellow suit sat forward. His long face took on a hard expression. "Now, I don't have to spell things out for people like yourselves. Some types one comes across can't seem to cut their way through any problem, and that does make things difficult. But you, I don't have to explain the situation to *you*. I've got what you want, and you've got what I want. Of course, you might find that child without me, but . . . you might not find her in time.

So: I want the wood and you want the child. It's a trade. A simple, clear-cut trade."

He looked around at the three shocked faces, and as if he were seeing nothing there but calm agreement, he smiled delightedly and rubbed his hands together. "Done and done," he said. "I knew right away, I said to myself, 'Now here is a group of intelligent, reasonable people!' I'm seldom wrong as a judge of character. Very seldom disappointed. So! All that remains is to write it up on paper, giving me the wood, and to sign it. It's best, don't you agree, to keep things legal and tidy. The rest is easy. Nothing to it. You go for your local constable, and he and I ride out and bring back the child *and* the criminals. No—oh, no, Mr. Foster—I understand your concern, but you mustn't come along. We'll do this business my way. There now! Your terrible ordeal is as good as over, isn't it? I'm so thankful I was here to help you out!"

16

The constable was fat, and he was sleepy. He wheezed when he spoke. And he spoke quite a bit as they started off, he and the man in the yellow suit. "First they roust me out of bed in the middle of the night, after I been out since sun-up looking for that child, and now I s'pose you're going to try to run me all the way," he said sourly. "I got to tell you this horse of mine is none too strong. I don't have to hurry her as a rule, so most of the time it don't matter. Seems to me we could've waited till dawn, anyway."

The man in the yellow suit was as courteous as always. "The Fosters have been waiting since yesterday morning," he pointed out. "Naturally, they're very upset. The sooner we get there, the sooner that child will be with them again."

"How come *you're* so deep in it?" asked the constable suspiciously. "Maybe you're in cahoots with the kidnappers, how do I know? You should of reported it right off, when you saw her get snatched."

The man in the yellow suit sighed. "But of course I had to find out where they were taking her," he explained patiently. "I came right back after that. And the Fosters are friends of mine. They've—uh—sold me their wood."

The constable's eyes went round. "I'll be!" he said. "What do you know about that! I didn't suppose they'd ever do a thing like that, friend or no friend. They're the first family around here, you know. Proud as peacocks, all of 'em. Family-proud, and land-proud, too. But they sold off, did they? Well, well." And he whistled in amazement.

They thumped along in silence for a while, out around the wood and across the star-lit meadow. Then the constable yawned deeply and said, "You ready to tell me how long this is going to take? How far we got to go?"

"Twenty miles north," said the man in the yellow suit.

The constable groaned. "Twenty miles!" He shifted the shotgun that rested across his saddle, and groaned again. "Clear up in the foothills? That's a fair way, all right."

There was no reply to this. The constable ran his fingers down the gleaming barrel of the shotgun.

Then he shrugged, and slumped a little in the saddle. "Might as well relax," he wheezed, suddenly companionable. "We'll be riding three, four hours."

Still there was no reply.

"Yessir," said the constable, trying again. "It's something new for these parts, kidnapping. Never had a case like this before that I know of, and I been in charge going on fifteen years."

He waited.

"You don't say so," his companion said at last.

"Yep, that's a fact," said the constable, with evident relief. Maybe now there would be some conversation! "Yep, fifteen years. Seen a lot of trouble in fifteen years, but nothing quite like this. 'Course, there's a first time for everything, as they say. We got a brand-new jailhouse, did you notice? Listen, it's a dandy! Give those folks nice clean accommodations." He chuckled. " 'Course, they won't be there long. Circuit judge'll be coming through next week. He'll send 'em over to Charleyville, most likely, to the county jail. That's what they do for your serious crimes. 'Course, we got a gallows of our own, if we ever need it. Keeps down trouble, *I* think, just having it there. Ain't ever used it yet. That's because they take care of the serious stuff over to Charleyville, like I say."

The constable paused to light a cigar, and went on cheerfully: "What you got planned for that piece of Foster land? Going to clear her? Put up a house, or a store, maybe?"

"No," said the man in the yellow suit.

The constable waited for more, but there was no more. His sour mood returned. He frowned and shook the ashes from his cigar. "Say," he said. "You're kind of a close-lipped feller, ain't you?"

The man in the yellow suit narrowed his eyes. His mouth, above the thin gray beard, twitched with annoyance. "Look here," he said tightly. "Would you mind if I rode on ahead? I'm worried about that child. I'll tell you how to get there, and I'll go on ahead and keep watch."

"Well," said the constable grudgingly, "all right, if you're in such a ding-danged hurry. But don't do nothing till I get there. Those folks are likely dangerous. I'll try to keep up, but this horse of mine, she's none too strong. Don't see as how I could get her to a gallop, even if I tried."

"That's right," said the man in the yellow suit. "So I'll go on ahead, and wait outside the house till you get there."

He explained the route carefully, then dug his heels into the flanks of the fat old horse, cantering off into the darkness where just a hint of dawn glowed on the edges of the hills far ahead.

The constable chewed on the end of his cigar. "Humph," he said to his horse. "Did you get a gander at that suit of clothes? Oh, well, it takes all kinds, as they say." And he followed slowly after, yawning, the gap between him and the man ahead lengthening with every mile.

17

For the second morning in a row, Winnie Foster woke early. Outside, in the ring of trees around the pond, the birds were celebrating, giving the new day a brass band's worth of greeting. Winnie freed herself from the twisted quilt and went to a window. Mist lay on the surface of the water, and the light was still pale. It looked unreal, and she felt, herself, unreal, waking where she had, with her hair wild and her dress all crumpled. She rubbed her eyes. Through the dewy weeds below the window, a toad hopped suddenly into view and Winnie peered at it eagerly. But no—of course it wasn't the same toad. And remembering that other toad—*her* toad, she thought now, almost fondly—it seemed to her that she had been away from home for weeks. Then she

heard a step on the loft stairs and thought, "Jesse!"
At once her cheeks flamed.

But it was Miles. He came into the parlor, and
when he saw that she was up, he smiled and whispered, "Good! You're awake. Come on—you can
help me catch some fish for breakfast."

This time, Winnie was careful not to make a noise
when she climbed into the rowboat. She made her
way to her seat in the stern, and Miles handed her
two old cane poles—"Watch out for the hooks!" he
warned—and a jar of bait: pork fat cut into little
pieces. A big brown night moth fluttered out from
under the oar blades propped beside her on the seat,
and wobbled off toward nowhere through the fra-
grant air. And from the bank, something plopped
into the water. A frog! Winnie caught just a glimpse
of it as it scissored away from shore. The water was
so clear that she could see tiny brown fish near the
bottom, flicking this way and that.

Miles pushed the rowboat off and sprang in, and
soon they were gliding up toward the near end of
the pond, where the water came in from the stream.
The locks grated as the oars dipped and swung, but
Miles was skillful. He rowed without a single splash.
The dripping from the blades, as they lifted, sent
rows of overlapping circles spreading silently behind
them. It was very peaceful. "They'll take me home

today," thought Winnie. She was somehow certain of this, and began to feel quite cheerful. She had been kidnapped, but nothing bad had happened, and now it was almost over. Now, remembering the visits of the night before, she smiled—and found that she loved them, this most peculiar family. They were her friends, after all. And hers alone.

"How'd you sleep?" Miles asked her.

"All right," she said.

"That's good. I'm glad. Ever been fishing before?"

"No," she told him.

"You'll like it. It's fun." And he smiled at her.

The mist was lifting now, as the sun poked up above the trees, and the water sparkled. Miles guided the rowboat near a spot where lily pads lay like up-turned palms on the surface. "We'll let her drift some here," he said. "There'll be trout down in those weeds and stems. Here—give me the poles and I'll bait the hooks for us."

Winnie sat watching him as he worked. His face was like Jesse's, and yet not like. It was thinner, without Jesse's rounded cheeks, and paler, and his hair was almost straight, clipped neatly below the ears. His hands were different, too, the fingers thicker, the skin scrubbed-looking, but black at the knuckles and under the nails. Winnie remembered then that he worked sometimes as a blacksmith, and indeed his shoulders, under his threadbare shirt, were broad and muscled. He looked solid, like an oar, whereas Jesse—well, she decided, Jesse was like water: thin, and quick.

Miles seemed to sense that she was watching him. He looked up from the bait jar and his eyes, returning her gaze, were soft. "Remember I told you I had two children?" he asked. "Well, one of 'em was a girl. I took her fishing, too." His face clouded then, and he shook his head. "Her name was Anna. Lord, how sweet she was, that child! It's queer to think she'd be close to eighty now, if she's even still alive. And my son—he'd be eighty-two."

Winnie looked at his young, strong face, and after a moment she said, "Why didn't you take them to the spring and give them some of the special water?"

"Well, of course, we didn't realize about the spring while we was still on the farm," said Miles. "Afterwards, I thought about going to find them. I wanted to, heaven knows. But, Winnie, how'd it have been if I had? My wife was nearly forty by then. And the children—well, what was the use? They'd have been near growed theirselves. They'd have had a pa close to the same age *they* was. No, it'd all have been so mixed up and peculiar, it just wouldn't have worked. Then Pa, he was dead-set against it, anyway. The fewer people know about the spring, he says, the fewer there are to tell about it. Here—here's your pole. Just ease the hook down in the water. You'll know when you get a bite."

Winnie clutched her pole, sitting sidewise in the stern, and watched the baited hook sink slowly down. A dragonfly, a brilliant blue jewel, darted up and paused over the lily pads, then swung up and away. From the nearest bank, a bullfrog spoke.

"There certainly are a lot of frogs around here," Winnie observed.

"That's so," said Miles. "They'll keep coming, too, long as the turtles stay away. Snappers, now, they'll eat a frog soon as look at him."

Winnie thought about this peril to the frogs, and sighed. "It'd be nice," she said, "if nothing ever had to die."

"Well, now, I don't know," said Miles. "If you think on it, you come to see there'd be so many creatures, including people, we'd all be squeezed in right up next to each other before long."

Winnie squinted at her fishing line and tried to picture a teeming world. "Mmm," she said, "yes, I guess you're right."

Suddenly the cane pole jerked in her hands and bent into an arch, its tip dragged down nearly to the water's surface. Winnie held on tight to the handle, her eyes wide.

"Hey!" cried Miles. "Look there! You got a bite. Fresh trout for breakfast, Winnie."

But just as suddenly the pole whipped straight again and the line went slack. "Shucks," said Miles. "It got away."

"I'm kind of glad," Winnie admitted, easing her rigid grip on the butt of the pole. "*You* fish, Miles. I'm not so sure I want to."

And so they drifted for a little longer. The sky was blue and hard now, the last of the mist dissolved, and the sun, stepping higher above the trees, was hot on Winnie's back. The first week of August was reasserting itself after a good night's sleep. It would be another searing day.

A mosquito appeared and sat down on Winnie's knee. She slapped at it absently, thinking about what Miles had said. If all the mosquitoes lived forever—and if they kept on having babies!—it would be terrible. The Tucks were right. It was best if no one knew about the spring, including the mosquitoes. She would keep the secret. She looked at Miles, and then she asked him, "What will you do, if you've got so much time?"

"Someday," said Miles, "I'll find a way to do something important."

Winnie nodded. That was what *she* wanted.

"The way I see it," Miles went on, "it's no good hiding yourself away, like Pa and lots of other people. And it's no good just thinking of your own pleasure, either. People got to do something useful if they're going to take up space in the world."

"But what will you *do?*" Winnie persisted.

"I don't know yet," said Miles. "I ain't had no schooling or nothing, and that makes it harder." Then he set his jaw and added, "I'll find a way, though. I'll locate something."

Winnie nodded. She reached out and ran her fingers across a lily pad that lay on the water beside the boat. It was warm and very dry, like a blotter, but near its center was a single drop of water, round and perfect. She touched the drop and brought her fingertip back wet; but the drop of water, though it rolled a little, remained as round and perfect as before.

And then Miles caught a fish. There it flopped, in the bottom of the boat, its jaw working, its gills fanning rapidly. Winnie drew up her knees and stared at it. It was beautiful, and horrible too, with gleaming, rainbow-colored scales, and an eye like a marble beginning to dim even as she watched it. The hook was caught in its upper lip, and suddenly Winnie wanted to weep. "Put it back, Miles," she said, her voice dry and harsh. "Put it back right away."

Miles started to protest, and then, looking at her face, he picked up the trout and gently worked the barbed hook free. "All right, Winnie," he said. He dropped the fish over the edge of the boat. It flipped its tail and disappeared under the lily pads.

"Will it be all right?" asked Winnie, feeling foolish and happy both at once.

"It'll be all right," Miles assured her. And then he said, "People got to be meat-eaters sometimes, though. It's the natural way. And that means killing things."

"I know," said Winnie weakly. "But still."

"Yes," said Miles. "I know."

18

And so there were flapjacks again for breakfast, but no one seemed to mind. "Didn't get a bite, eh?" said Mae.

"No," said Miles, "nothing we wanted to keep."

That was true, anyway. And though Winnie blushed as he said it, she was grateful that he didn't explain.

"Never mind," said Mae. "You're likely out of practice. Tomorrow, maybe."

"Sure," said Miles. "Tomorrow."

But it was the thought of seeing Jesse again that kept Winnie's stomach fluttering. And at last he came down from the loft, yawning and rosy, rubbing his curls, just as Mae was piling the plates with flapjacks. "Well, slug-a-bed," she said to him fondly. "You come near to missing breakfast. Miles and Winnie been up for hours, out fishing and back already."

"Oh?" said Jesse, his eyes on Miles. "Where's the fish, then? How come we got nothing but flapjacks?"

"No luck," said Mae. "They wasn't biting, for some reason."

"Reason is, Miles don't know how to fish," said Jesse. He grinned at Winnie and she lowered her eyes, her heart thumping.

"It don't matter," said Mae. "We got plenty without. Come and get your plates, everybody."

They sat about in the parlor, as they had the night before. The ceiling swam with bright reflections, and sunlight streamed across the dusty, chip-strewn floor. Mae surveyed it all and sighed contentedly. "Now, this is real nice," she said, her fork poised above her plate. "Everyone sitting down together. And having Winnie here—why, it's just like a party."

"That's the truth," said Jesse and Miles both together, and Winnie felt a rush of happiness.

"Still, we got things to discuss," Tuck reminded them. "There's the business of the horse getting stole. And we got to get Winnie home where she belongs. How we going to do that without the horse?"

"After breakfast, Tuck," said Mae firmly. "Don't spoil a good meal with a lot of talk. We'll get to it soon enough."

So they were silent, eating, and this time Winnie

licked the syrup from her fingers without pausing to think about it first. Her fears at last night's supper seemed silly to her now. Perhaps they *were* crazy, but they weren't criminals. She loved them. They belonged to her.

Tuck said, "How'd you sleep, child?"

And she answered, "Just fine," and wished, for a fleeting moment, that she could stay with them forever in that sunny, untidy little house by the pond. Grow up with them and perhaps, if it was true about the spring—then perhaps, when she was seventeen . . . She glanced at Jesse, where he sat on the floor, his curly head bent over his plate. Then she looked at Miles. And then her eyes went to Tuck and lingered on his sad, creased face. It occurred to her that he was the dearest of them all, though she couldn't have explained why she felt that way.

However, there wasn't time to wonder, for at that moment someone knocked at the door.

It was such an alien sound, so sudden and surprising, that Mae dropped her fork, and everyone looked up, startled. "Who's that?" said Tuck.

"I can't imagine," whispered Mae. "We ain't never had callers in all the years we been here."

The knock came again.

"I'll go, Ma," said Miles.

"No, stay where you are," she said. "*I'll* go." She

put her plate down carefully on the floor and stood up, straightening her skirts. Then she went to the kitchen and opened the door.

Winnie recognized the voice at once. It was a rich and pleasant voice. The man in the yellow suit. And he was saying, "Good morning, Mrs. Tuck. It *is* Mrs. Tuck, isn't it. May I come in?"

19

The man in the yellow suit came into the sunlit parlor. He stood for a moment, looking around at them all, Mae and Miles and Jesse and Tuck, and Winnie, too. His face was without expression, but there was something unpleasant behind it that Winnie sensed at once, something that made her instantly suspicious. And yet his voice was mild when he said, "You're safe now, Winifred. I've come to take you home."

"We was going to bring her back directly, ourself," said Tuck, standing up slowly. "She ain't been in no danger."

"You're Mr. Tuck, I suppose," said the man in the yellow suit.

"I am," said Tuck formally, his back straighter than usual.

"Well, you may as well sit down again. You, too, Mrs. Tuck. I have a great deal to say and very little time for saying it."

Mae sat down on the edge of the rocker, and Tuck sat, too, but his eyes were narrowed.

Jesse said, uneasily, "Who in tarnation do you think you—"

But Tuck interrupted. "Hush, boy. Let him speak his piece."

"That's wise," said the man in the yellow suit. "I'll be as brief as possible." He took off his hat and laid it on the mantel, and then he stood tapping his foot on the littered hearth, facing them. His face was smooth and empty. "I was born west of here," he began, "and all the time I was growing up, my grandmother told me stories. They were wild, unbelievable stories, but *I* believed them. They involved a dear friend of my grandmother's who married into a very odd family. Married the older of two sons, and they had two children. It was after the children were born that she began to see that the family was odd. This friend of my grandmother's, she lived with her husband for twenty years, and strange to say, he never got any older. *She* did, but he didn't. And neither did his mother or his father or his brother. People began to wonder about that family, and my grandmother's friend decided at last that they were witches, or worse. She left her husband and came with her children to live at my grandmother's house for a short while. Then she moved west. I don't know what became of her. But my mother still remembers playing with the children. They were all about the same age. There was a son, and a daughter."

"Anna!" whispered Miles.

Mae burst out, "You got no call to come and bring us pain!"

And Tuck added roughly, "You got something to say, you better come to the point and say it."

"There, there, now," said the man in the yellow suit. He spread his long, white fingers in a soothing gesture. "Hear me out. As I've told you, I was fascinated by my grandmother's stories. People who never grew older! It was fantastic. It took possession of me. I decided to devote my life to finding out if it could be true, and if so, how and why. I went to school, I went to a university, I studied philosophy, metaphysics, even a little medicine. None of it did me any good. Oh, there were ancient legends, but nothing more. I nearly gave it up. It began to seem ridiculous, and a waste of time. I went home. My grandmother was very old by then. I took her a present one day, a music box. And when I gave it to her, it reminded her of something: the woman, the mother of the family that didn't grow old, *she* had had a music box."

Mae's hand went to the pocket of her skirt. Her

mouth opened, and then she shut it again with a snap.

"That music box played a very particular tune," the man in the yellow suit went on. "My grandmother's friend and her children—Anna? Was that the daughter's name?—they'd heard it so often that they knew it by heart. They'd taught it to my mother during the short time they lived in the house. We talked about it then, all those years afterward, my mother, my grandmother, and I. My mother was able to remember the melody, finally. She taught it to me. That was nearly twenty years ago now, but I kept it in my head. It was a clue."

The man in the yellow suit folded his arms and rocked a little. His voice was easy, almost friendly. "During those twenty years," he said, "I worked at other things. But I couldn't forget the tune or the family that didn't grow older. They haunted my dreams. So a few months ago I left my home and I started out to look for them, following the route they were said to have taken when they left their farm. No one I asked along the way knew anything. No one had heard of them, no one recognized their name. But two evenings ago, I heard that music box, I heard that very tune, and it was coming from the Fosters' wood. And next morning early, I saw the family at last, taking Winifred away. I followed, and I heard their story, every word."

Mae's face drained of color. Her mouth hung open. And Tuck said hoarsely, "What you going to do?"

The man in the yellow suit smiled. "The Fosters have given me the wood," he said. "In exchange for bringing Winifred home. I was the only one who knew where she was, you see. So it was a trade. Yes, I followed you, Mrs. Tuck, and then I took your horse and went directly back."

The tension in the parlor was immense. Winnie found that she could scarcely breathe. It *was* true, then! Or was the man who stood there crazy, too?

"Horse thief!" cried Tuck. "Get to the point! What you going to do?"

"It's very simple," said the man in the yellow suit. And, as he said this, the smoothness of his face began to loosen a little. A faint flush crept up his neck, and the pitch of his voice lifted, became a fraction higher. "Like all magnificent things, it's very simple. The wood—and the spring—belong to me now." He patted his breast pocket. "I have a paper here, all signed and legal, to prove it. I'm going to sell the water, you see."

"You can't do that!" roared Tuck. "You got to be out of your mind!"

The man in the yellow suit frowned. "But I'm not going to sell it to just anybody," he protested. "Only to certain people, people who deserve it. And it will be very, very expensive. But who wouldn't give a fortune to live forever?"

"I wouldn't," said Tuck grimly.

"Exactly," said the man in the yellow suit. His eyes glowed. "Ignorant people like you should never have the opportunity. It should be kept for . . . certain others. And for me. However, since it's already too late to keep you out, you may as well join me in what I'm going to do. You can show me where the spring is and help me to advertise. We'll set up demonstrations. You know—things that would be fatal to anybody else, but won't affect you in the least. I'll pay for your assistance, of course. It won't take long for the word to spread. And then you can go your way. Well, what do you say?"

Jesse said dully, "Freaks. You want us to be freaks. In a patent-medicine show."

The man in the yellow suit raised his eyebrows and a nervous petulance came into his voice. "Of course, if the idea doesn't appeal to you," he said, blinking rapidly, "you needn't be in on it. I can find the spring and manage just as well without you. But it seemed the gentlemanly thing to make the offer. After all," he added, looking round at the cluttered room, "it would mean you could afford to live like people again, instead of pigs."

And that was when the tension burst. All four Tucks sprang to their feet at once, while Winnie, very frightened, shrank back in her chair. Tuck cried, "You're a madman! A loony! You can't let *no* one know about that water. Don't you see what would *happen?*"

"I've given you your chance," shrilled the man in the yellow suit, "and you've refused it." He seized Winnie roughly by the arm and dragged her up out of her chair. "I'll take the child, and be on about my business."

Tuck began to rave now, his face stretched with horror. "Madman!" he shouted. And Miles and Jesse began to shout, too. They crowded after as the man in the yellow suit dragged Winnie through the kitchen to the door.

"No!" she was screaming, for now at last she hated him. "I won't go with you! I won't!"

But he opened the door and pushed her out in front of him. His eyes were like blind firepoints, his face was twisted.

Then the shouting behind them stopped abruptly, and in the midst of the sudden silence came Mae's voice, flat and cold. "You leave that child be," she said.

Winnie stared. Mae was standing just outside the doorway. She held Tuck's long-forgotten shotgun by the barrel, like a club.

The man in the yellow suit smiled a ghastly smile. "I can't think why you're so upset. Did you really believe you could keep that water for yourselves? Your selfishness is really quite extraordinary, and worse than that, you're stupid. You could have done what I'm about to do, long ago. Now it's too late. Once Winifred drinks some of the water, she'll do just as well for my demonstrations. Even better. Children are much more appealing, anyway. So you may as well relax. There's nothing you can do to stop me."

But he was wrong. Mae lifted the shotgun. Behind her, Miles gasped, "Ma! *No!*"

But Mae's face was dark red. "Not Winnie!" she said between clenched teeth. "You ain't going to do a thing like that to Winnie. And you ain't going to give out the secret." Her strong arms swung the shotgun round her head, like a wheel. The man in the yellow suit jerked away, but it was too late. With a dull cracking sound, the stock of the shotgun smashed into the back of his skull. He dropped like a tree, his face surprised, his eyes wide open. And at that very moment, riding through the pine trees just in time to see it all, came the Treegap constable.

20

Winnie was standing with her cheek pressed into Tuck's chest, her arms flung tight around him. She trembled, and kept her eyes squeezed shut. She could feel Tuck's breath come and go in little gasps. It was very quiet.

The Treegap constable knelt over the sprawled body of the man in the yellow suit, and then he said, "He ain't dead. Leastways, not yet."

Winnie opened her eyes a crack. She could see the shotgun lying on the grass where Mae had dropped it. She could see Mae's hands, too, hanging limp, clenching, then hanging limp again. The sun was scorching hot, and near her ear a gnat whined.

The constable stood up. "What did you hit him for?" he wheezed resentfully.

"He was taking the child away," said Mae. Her

voice was dull and exhausted. "He was taking the child against her will."

At this the constable exploded. "Ding-dang it, woman, what you trying to say? Taking that child against her will? That's what *you* done. You *kidnapped* that child."

Winnie let go of Tuck's waist and turned around. Her trembling had stopped. "They didn't kidnap me," she said. "I came because I wanted to."

Behind her, Tuck drew his breath in sharply.

"You wanted to?" echoed the constable, his eyes wide with disbelief. "You *wanted* to?"

"That's right," said Winnie unflinchingly. "They're my friends."

The constable stared at her. He scratched his chin, eyebrows high, and eased his own shotgun to the ground. Then he shrugged and looked down at the man in the yellow suit, who lay motionless on the grass, the blazing sun white on his face and hands. His eyes were closed now, but except for that, he looked more than ever like a marionette, a marionette flung carelessly into a corner, arms and legs every which way midst tangled strings.

The one glance she gave him fixed his appearance forever in Winnie's mind. She turned her eyes away quickly, looking to Tuck for relief. But Tuck was not looking back at her. Instead, he was gazing at the body on the ground, leaning forward slightly, his brows drawn down, his mouth a little open. It was as if he were entranced and—yes, envious—like a starving man looking through a window at a banquet. Winnie could not bear to see him like that. She reached out a hand and touched him, and it broke the spell. He blinked and took her hand, squeezing it.

"Well, anyway," said the constable at last, turning businesslike, "I got to take charge here. Get this feller into the house before he fries. I'm telling you now: if he don't make it, you're in a pickle, you people. Now, here's what we'll do. You," he said, pointing at Mae, "you got to come with me, you and the little girl. You got to be locked up right away; and the little girl, I got to get her home. The rest of you, you stay here with him. Look after him. I'll get back with a doctor quick as I can. Should have brought a deputy, but I didn't expect nothing like this to happen. Well, it's too late now. All right, let's get moving."

Miles said softly, "Ma. We'll get you out right away."

"Sure, Ma," said Jesse.

"Don't worry about me none," said Mae in the same exhausted voice. "I'll make out."

"Make out?" exclaimed the constable. "You people beat all. If this feller dies, you'll get the gallows, that's what you'll get, if that's what you mean by make out."

Tuck's face crumpled. "The gallows?" he whispered. "Hanging?"

"That's it," said the constable. "That's the law. Now, let's get going."

Miles and Jesse lifted the man in the yellow suit and carried him carefully into the house, but Tuck stood staring, and Winnie could guess what he was thinking. The constable swung her up onto his horse and directed Mae to her own saddle. But Winnie kept her eyes on Tuck. His face was very pale, the creases deeper than ever, and his eyes looked blank and sunken. She heard him whisper again, "The gallows!"

And then Winnie said something she had never said before, but the words were words she had sometimes heard, and often longed to hear. They sounded strange on her own lips and made her sit up straighter. "Mr. Tuck," she said, "don't worry. Everything's going to be all right."

The constable glanced heavenward and shook his head. Then, clutching his shotgun, he climbed up behind Winnie and turned the horse toward the path. "You first," he barked at Mae. "I got to keep an eye on you. And as for you," he added grimly, speaking to Tuck, "you better hope that feller don't die on you. I'll be back soon as I can."

"Everything'll be all right," Tuck repeated slowly.

Mae, slumped on the back of the fat old horse, did

not respond. But Winnie leaned round the constable and looked back at Tuck. "You'll see," she said. And then she faced forward, sitting very straight. She was going home, but the thought of that was far from her mind. She watched the rump of the horse ahead, the swish of coarse, dusty hairs as he moved his tail. And she watched the swaying, sagging back of the woman who rode him.

Up through the dim pine trees they went, the constable's breath wheezing in her ears, and emerging from the coolness and the green, Winnie saw again the wide world spread before her, shimmering with light and possibility. But the possibilities were different now. They did not point to what might happen to her but to what she herself might keep from happening. For the only thing she could think of was the clear and terrible necessity: Mae Tuck must never go to the gallows. Whatever happened to the man in the yellow suit, Mae Tuck must not be hanged. Because if all they had said was true, then Mae, even if she were the cruelest of murderers and deserved to be put to death—Mae Tuck would not be able to die.

21

Winnie pulled her little rocking chair up to her bedroom window and sat down. The rocking chair had
been given to her when she was very small, but she
still squeezed into it sometimes, when no one was
looking, because the rocking made her almost remember something pleasant, something soothing,
that would never quite come up to the surface of her
mind. And tonight she wanted to be soothed.

The constable had brought her home. They had
seized her at once, flinging the gate open and swooping down on her, her mother weeping, her father
speechless, hugging her to him, her grandmother
babbling with excitement. There was a painful pause
when the constable told them she had gone away of
her own free will, but it only lasted for a moment.
They did not, would not believe it, and her grand-

mother said, "It was the elves. We heard them. They must have bewitched her."

And so they had borne her into the house, and after she had taken the bath they insisted upon, they fed and petted her and refused, with little laughs and murmurs, to accept her answers to their questions: She had gone away with the Tucks because— well, she just wanted to. The Tucks had been very kind to her, had given her flapjacks, taken her fishing. The Tucks were good and gentle people. All this would have been swept away in any case, however, this good impression of her friends which she was trying to create, when she told them what had happened to the man in the yellow suit. Had they really given him the wood in exchange for finding her? They had. Well, perhaps he wouldn't want it now. Mae had hit him with the shotgun. He was very sick. They received this news with mingled hope and horror, and her father said, "I suppose the wood will be ours again if that man should . . . that is, if he doesn't . . ."

"You mean, if he dies," Winnie had said, flatly, and they had sat back, shocked. Soon after, they put her to bed, with many kisses. But they peered at her anxiously over their shoulders as they tiptoed out of her bedroom, as if they sensed that she was different now from what she had been before. As if some part of her had slipped away.

Well, thought Winnie, crossing her arms on the windowsill, she *was* different. Things had happened to her that were hers alone, and had nothing to do with them. It was the first time. And no amount of telling about it could help them understand or share what she felt. It was satisfying and lonely, both at once. She rocked, gazing out at the twilight, and the soothing feeling came reliably into her bones. That feeling—it tied her to them, to her mother, her father, her grandmother, with strong threads too ancient and precious to be broken. But there were new threads now, tugging and insistent, which tied her just as firmly to the Tucks.

Winnie watched the sky slide into blackness over the wood outside her window. There was not the least hint of a breeze to soften the heavy August night. And then, over the treetops, on the faraway horizon, there was a flash of white. Heat lightning. Again and again it throbbed, without a sound. It was like pain, she thought. And suddenly she longed for a thunderstorm.

She cradled her head in her arms and closed her eyes. At once the image of the man in the yellow suit rose up. She could see him again, sprawled motionless on the sun-blanched grass. "He can't die," she whispered, thinking of Mae. "He mustn't." And then she considered his plans for the water in the spring, and Tuck's voice saying, "They'd all come running like pigs to slops." And she found herself thinking, "If it's true about the spring, then he has to die. He must. And that's why she did it."

Then she heard hoofbeats on the road below, a horse hurrying into the village, and not long after, there were footsteps and a knocking on the door. Winnie crept out of her room and crouched in the shadows at the top of the stairs. It was the constable. She heard him saying, "So that's that, Mr. Foster. We can't press no kidnapping charges, since your little girl claims there *wasn't* no kidnapping. But it don't matter now, anyway. The doc just got back a few minutes ago. That feller—the one you sold your land to? He's dead." There was a pause, and the murmur of other voices; then a match striking, the acrid smell of fresh cigar smoke. "Yep, she got him a good one, all right. He never even come to. So it's an open-and-shut case, since I seen her do it. Eyewitness. No question about it. They'll hang her for sure."

Winnie went back to her room and climbed into bed. She lay in the dark, propped up on the pillows, and stared at the lighter square of her window, at the heat lightning throbbing. It was like pain, she thought again, a dull pain on the fringes of the sky. Mae had killed the man in the yellow suit. And she had meant to kill him.

Winnie had killed a wasp once, in fear and anger, just in time to spare herself a stinging. She had slammed at the wasp with a heavy book, and killed it. And then, seeing its body broken, the thin wings stilled, she had wished it were alive again. She had wept for that wasp. Was Mae weeping now for the man in the yellow suit? In spite of her wish to spare the world, did she wish he were alive again? There was no way of knowing. But Mae had done what she thought she had to do. Winnie closed her eyes to shut out the silent pulsing of the lightning. Now *she* would have to do something. She had no idea what, but something. Mae Tuck must not go to the gallows.

22

Next morning Winnie went out to the fence directly after breakfast. It was the hottest day yet, so heavy that the slightest exertion brought on a flood of perspiration, an exhaustion in the joints. Two days before, they would have insisted that she stay indoors, but now, this morning, they were careful with her, a little gingerly, as if she were an egg. She had said, "I'm going outside now," and they had said, "All right, but come in if it gets too hot, won't you, dear?" And she had answered, "Yes."

The earth, where it was worn bald under the gate, was cracked, and hard as rock, a lifeless tan color; and the road was an aisle of brilliant velvet dust. Winnie leaned against the fence, her hands gripping the warm metal of the bars, and thought about Mae behind another set of bars in the jailhouse. And then, lifting her head, she saw the toad. It was squatting where she had seen it first, across the road. "Hello!" she said, very glad to see it.

The toad did not so much as flick a muscle or blink an eye. It looked dried out today, parched. "It's thirsty," said Winnie to herself. "No wonder, on a day like this." She left the fence and went back into the cottage. "Granny, can I have some water in a dish? There's a toad out front that looks as if he's just about to die of thirst."

"A toad?" said her grandmother, wrinkling her nose in disgust. "Nasty things, toads."

"Not this one," said Winnie. "This one is always out there, and I like him. Can I give him a drink of water?"

"Toads don't drink water, Winifred. It wouldn't do him any good."

"They don't drink water at all?"

"No. They take it in through their skins, like a sponge. When it rains."

"But it hasn't rained forever!" said Winnie, alarmed. "I could sprinkle some water on him, couldn't I? That would help, wouldn't it?"

"Well, I suppose so," said her grandmother. "Where is he? In the yard?"

"No," said Winnie. "He's across the road."

"I'll come with you, then. I don't want you leaving the yard alone."

But when they came out to the fence, Winnie balancing a small bowl of water with enormous care, the toad was gone.

"Well, he must be all right," said her grandmother. "If he could hop off."

With mingled disappointment and relief, Winnie tipped the water onto the cracked earth at the gate. It was sucked in immediately, and the wet brown stain it left behind paled and vanished almost as quickly.

"I never saw such heat in all my life," said Winnie's grandmother, dabbing uselessly at her neck with a handkerchief. "Don't stay out here much longer."

"I won't," said Winnie, and was left alone once more. She sat down on the grass and sighed. Mae! What could she do to set Mae free? She closed her eyes against the glaring light, and watched, a little dizzily, as brilliant patterns of red and orange danced inside her eyelids.

And then, miraculously, Jesse was there, crouching just on the other side of the fence. "Winnie!" he hissed. "You sleeping?"

"Oh, Jesse!" Her eyes flew open and she reached through the fence to grasp his hand. "I'm so glad to see you! What can we do? We have to get her out!"

"Miles's got a plan, but I don't see how it can work," said Jesse, speaking quickly, his voice almost a whisper. "He knows a lot about carpentering. He says he can take Ma's window frame right straight out of the wall, bars and all, and she can climb through. We're going to try it tonight when it gets dark. Only trouble is, that constable keeps watching her every minute, he's so durned proud of having a prisoner in that new jail of his. We been down to see her. She's all right. But even if she can climb through the window, he'll come after her soon's he sees she's gone. Seems to me he'll notice right off. That don't give us much time to get away. But we got to try it. There ain't no other way. Anyhow, I come to say goodbye. We won't be able to come back here for a long, long time, Winnie, if we get away. I mean, they'll be looking for Ma. Winnie, listen—I won't see you again, not for ages. Look now—here's a bottle of water from the spring. You keep it. And then, no matter where you are, when you're seventeen, Winnie, you can drink it, and then come find us. We'll leave directions somehow. Winnie, please say you will!"

He pressed the little bottle into her hands and Winnie took it, closing her fingers over it. "Jesse, wait!" she whispered breathlessly, for all at once she had the answer. "I can help! When your mother climbs out the window, I'll climb in and take her place. I can wrap myself up in her blanket, and when the constable looks in, he won't be able to tell the difference. Not in the dark. I can hump up and look a lot bigger. Miles can even put the window back.

That would give you time to get away! You'd have at least till morning!"

Jesse squinted at her, and then he said, "Yep—you know, it might work. It might just make the difference. But I don't know as Pa's going to want you taking any risk. I mean, what'll they say to you after, when they find out?"

"I don't know," said Winnie, "but it doesn't matter. Tell your father I want to help. I *have* to help. If it wasn't for me, there wouldn't have been any trouble in the first place. Tell him I have to."

"Well . . . all right. Can you get out after dark?"

"Yes," said Winnie.

"Then—at midnight, Winnie. I'll be waiting for you right here at midnight."

"Winifred!" an anxious voice called from the cottage. "Who's that you're talking to?"

Winnie stood up and turned to answer. "It's just a boy, Granny. I'll be in in a minute." When she turned around again, Jesse was gone. Winnie clutched the little bottle in her hands and tried to control the rising excitement that made her breath catch. At midnight she would make a difference in the world.

23

It was the longest day: mindlessly hot, unspeakably hot, too hot to move or even think. The countryside, the village of Treegap, the wood—all lay defeated. Nothing stirred. The sun was a ponderous circle without edges, a roar without a sound, a blazing glare so thorough and remorseless that even in the Fosters' parlor, with curtains drawn, it seemed an actual presence. You could not shut it out.

Winnie's mother and grandmother sat plaintive all afternoon in the parlor, fanning themselves and sipping lemonade, their hair unsettled and their knees loose. It was totally unlike them, this lapse from gentility, and it made them much more interesting. But Winnie didn't stay with them. Instead, she took her own brimming glass to her room and sat in her little rocker by the window. Once she had hidden Jesse's bottle in a bureau drawer, there was nothing to do but wait. In the hall outside her room, the grandfather's clock ticked deliberately, unimpressed with anyone's impatience, and Winnie found herself rocking to its rhythm—forward, back, forward, back, tick, tock, tick, tock. She tried to read, but it was so quiet that she could not concentrate, and so she was glad when at last it was time for supper. It was something to do, though none of them could manage more than a nibble.

But later, when Winnie went out again to the fence, she saw that the sky was changing. It was not so much clouding up as thickening, somehow, from every direction at once, the blank blue gone to haze. And then, as the sun sank reluctantly behind the treetops, the haze hardened to a brilliant brownish-yellow. In the wood, the leaves turned underside-up, giving the trees a silvery cast.

The air was noticeably heavier. It pressed on Winnie's chest and made her breathing difficult. She turned and went back into the cottage. "It's going to rain, I think," she told the prostrate group in the parlor, and the news was received with little moans of gratitude.

Everyone went to bed early, closing windows firmly on their way. For outside, though it was almost dark, shreds of the hard brown-yellow light lingered on the rims of things, and there was a wind beginning, small gusts that rattled the fence gate and set the trees to rustling. The smell of rain hung sweet in the air. "What a week *this* has been!" said Winnie's grandmother. "Well, thank the Lord, it's almost over." And Winnie thought to herself: Yes, it's almost over.

There were three hours to wait before midnight and nothing whatever to do. Winnie wandered restlessly about her room, sat in her rocker, lay on her bed, counted the ticks of the hall clock. Beneath her excitement, she was thick with guilt. For the second time in three short days—though they seemed many more than that—she was about to do something which she knew would be forbidden. She didn't have to ask.

Winnie had her own strong sense of rightness. She knew that she could always say, afterward, "Well, you never told me *not* to!" But how silly that would be! Of course it would never occur to them to include such a thing on their list of don'ts. She could hear them saying it, and almost smiled: "Now, remember, Winifred—don't bite your fingernails, don't interrupt when someone else is speaking, and don't go down to the jailhouse at midnight to change places with prisoners."

Still, it wasn't really funny. What would happen in the morning, when the constable found her in the cell and had to bring her home for the second time? What would they say? Would they ever trust her again? Winnie squirmed, sitting in the rocker, and swallowed uncomfortably. Well, she would have to make them understand, somehow, without explaining.

The hall clock chimed eleven. Outside, the wind had stopped. Everything, it seemed, was waiting. Winnie lay down and closed her eyes. Thinking of Tuck and Mae, of Miles and Jesse, her heart softened. They needed her. To take care of them. For in the funny sort of way that had struck her at the first, they were helpless. Or too trusting. Well, *something* like that. Anyway, they needed her. She would not disappoint them. Mae would go free. No one would have to find out—Winnie would not have to find out—that Mae could not . . . but Winnie blocked the picture from her mind, the horror that would prove the secret. Instead, she turned her thoughts to Jesse. When she was seventeen—would she? If it was true, would she? And if she did, would she be sorry afterwards? Tuck had said, "It's something you don't find out how you feel until afterwards." But no—it wasn't true. She knew that, now, here in her own bedroom. They were probably crazy after all. But she loved them anyway. They needed her. And, thinking this, Winnie fell asleep.

She woke with a jerk sometime later, and sat up,

alarmed. The clock was ticking steadily, the darkness was complete. Outside, the night seemed poised
on tiptoe, waiting, waiting, holding its breath for
the storm. Winnie stole out to the hall and frowned
at the clock face in the shadows. And at last she could
make it out, for the black Roman numerals were
just barely visible against their white ground, the
brass hands glowed faintly. As she peered at them,
the long hand snapped forward one more notch, with
a loud click. She had not missed her moment—it was
five minutes to midnight.

24

Leaving the house was so easy that Winnie felt faintly shocked. She had half expected that the instant she put a foot on the stairs they would leap from their beds and surround her with accusations. But no one stirred. And she was struck by the realization that, if she chose, she could slip out night after night without their knowing. The thought made her feel more guilty than ever that she should once more take advantage of their trust. But tonight, this one last time, she had to. There was no other way. She opened the door and slipped out into the heavy August night.

Leaving the cottage was like leaving something real and moving into dream. Her body felt weightless, and she seemed to float down the path to the gate. Jesse was there, waiting. Neither of them spoke. He took her hand and they ran together, lightly, down the road, past other sleeping cottages, into the dim and empty center of the village. The big glass windows here were lidded eyes that didn't care—that barely saw them, barely gave them back reflections. The blacksmith's shop, the mill, the church, the stores, so busy and alive in daylight, were hunched, deserted now, dark piles and shapes without a purpose or a meaning. And then, ahead, Winnie saw the jailhouse, its new wood still unpainted, lamplight spilling through a window at the front. And there, in the cleared yard behind it, like a great L upside down, was the gallows.

The sky flashed white. But this time it wasn't heat lightning, for a few moments later a low mumble, still far away, announced at last the coming storm. A fresh breeze lifted Winnie's hair, and from somewhere in the village behind them a dog barked.

Two shadows detached themselves from the gloom as Winnie and Jesse came up. Tuck pulled her to him and hugged her hard, and Miles squeezed her hand. No one said a word. Then the four of them crept to the back of the building. Here, too high for Winnie to see into, was a barred window through which, from the room in front, light glowed faintly. Winnie peered up at it, at the blackness of the bars with the dim gold of the light between. Into her head came lines from an old poem:

Stone walls do not a prison make,
Nor iron bars a cage.

Over and over the lines repeated themselves in her head till they were altogether meaningless. Another roll of thunder sounded. The storm was moving nearer.

Then Miles was standing on a box. He was pouring oil around the frame of the window. A swirl of wind brought the thick, rich smell of it down to Winnie's nostrils. Tuck handed up a tool and Miles began to pry at the nails securing the window frame. Miles knew carpentering. Miles could do the job. Winnie shivered and held tight to Jesse's hand. One nail was free. Another. Tuck reached up to receive them as they came out one by one. A fourth nail screeched as it was pried up, and Miles poured on more oil.

From the front of the jailhouse, the constable yawned noisily and began to whistle. The whistling came nearer. Miles dropped down. They heard the constable's footsteps coming up to Mae's cell. The barred door clanked. Then the footsteps receded, the whistling grew fainter. An inner door shut, and the lamp glow disappeared.

At once Miles was up again and prying at the nails. An eighth was out, a ninth, a tenth. Winnie counted carefully, while behind her counting, her mind sang, "Stone walls do not a prison make."

Miles handed down the prying tool. He grasped the bars of the window firmly, ready to pull, and stood poised. "What is he waiting for?" thought Winnie. "Why doesn't he . . ." Then—a flash of lightning and, soon after, a crack of thunder. In the midst of the noise, Miles gave a mighty heave. But the window did not budge.

The thunder ebbed. Winnie's heart sank. What if it was all impossible? What if the window would never come out? What if . . . She looked over her shoulder at the dark shape of the gallows, and shuddered.

Again a flash of lightning, and this time a crashing burst of noise from the swirling sky. Miles yanked. The window frame sprang free, and still grasping it by the bars, he tumbled backward off the box. The job was done.

Two arms appeared in the hole left by the missing frame. Mae! Her head appeared. It was too dark to see her face. The window—what if it was too small for her to squeeze through? What if . . . But now her shoulders were out. She groaned softly. Another flash of lightning lit her face for an instant and Winnie saw an expression there of deep concentration, tip of tongue protruding, brows furrowed.

Now Tuck was on the box, helping her, giving her his own shoulders to pull on, Miles and Jesse close at his sides, arms upstretched, eager to receive her bulk. Her hips were free—now, look out!—here she came, her skirts tearing on the rough edges of the boards, arms flailing—and they were all in a heap on the ground. Another crash of thunder muffled Jesse's bursting, exultant laugh. Mae was free.

Winnie clasped her trembling hands thankfully. And then the first drop of rain plopped precisely on the tip of her nose. The Tucks untangled themselves and turned to her. One by one, as the rain began, they drew her to them and kissed her. One by one she kissed them back. Was it rain on Mae's face? On Tuck's? Or was it tears? Jesse was last. He put his arms around her and hugged her tight, and whispered the single word, "Remember!"

Then Miles was on the box again, lifting her. Her hands grasped the edges of the window. This time she waited with him. When the thunder came, it tore the sky apart with its roar, and as it came, she pulled herself through, and dropped to the cot inside, unharmed. She looked up at the open square and saw the frame with Miles's hands holding it. The next obliging roll of thunder saw it wedged once more into place. And then—would Miles put back the nails? She waited.

Rain came in sheets now, riding the wind, flung crosswise through the night. Lightning crackled, a brilliant, jagged streak, and thunder rattled the little building. The tension in the parched earth eased and vanished. Winnie felt it go. The muscles of her stomach loosened, and all at once she was exhausted.

Still she waited. Would Miles put back the nails? At last, standing tiptoe on the cot, she grasped the bars of the window, pulling herself up till she could just see through. Rain blew into her face, but at the next flash of lightning, looking down, she saw that the yard was empty. And before the thunder followed, in a pause while wind and rain held back for one brief moment, she thought she heard, fading in the distance, the tinkling little melody of the music box. The Tucks—her darling Tucks—were gone.

25

The first week of August was long over. And now, though autumn was still some weeks away, there was a feeling that the year had begun its downward arc, that the wheel was turning again, slowly now, but soon to go faster, turning once more in its changeless sweep of change. Winnie, standing at the fence in front of the touch-me-not cottage, could hear the new note in the voices of the birds. Whole clouds of them lifted, chattering, into the sky above the wood, and then settled, only to lift again. Across the road, goldenrod was coming into bloom. And an early-drying milkweed had opened its rough pod, exposing a host of downy-headed seeds. As she watched, one of these detached itself into a sudden breeze and sailed sedately off, while others leaned from the pod as if to observe its departure.

Winnie dropped down cross-legged on the grass. Two weeks had gone by since the night of the storm, the night of Mae Tuck's escape. And Mae had not been found. There was no trace of her at all, or of Tuck or Miles or Jesse. Winnie was profoundly grateful for that. But she was also profoundly tired. It had been a trying two weeks.

For the hundredth time she reviewed it all: how the constable had come into the cell soon after she had settled herself on the cot; how he had let down a shutter over the window to keep out the rain; how, then, he had stood over her as she hunched under the blanket, her breath heavy, trying to look as large as possible; how, finally, he had gone away and not come back till morning.

But she had not dared to sleep, for fear she would kick off the blanket and give herself away—give the Tucks away—unwittingly. So she had lain there, pulse thudding, eyes wide open. She would never forget the rattle of the rain on the jailhouse roof, or the smell of wet wood, or the darkness that had saved them all; or how difficult it was not to cough. She had wanted to cough as soon as it occurred to her that she mustn't, and she passed a long hour trying to swallow away the tickle that perversely constricted her throat. And she would never forget the crash outside that made her heart race, that she could not investigate, and did not understand till morning, when on the way home she saw that the gallows had blown over in the wind.

But oh!—it made her tremble still to remember the constable's face when he found her. She had heard first a bustling in the front of the jail, and smelled fresh coffee, and had sat up, stiff with apprehension. Then the inner door opened—the door, she now saw, which separated the office from the pair of cells—and in the light that streamed before him, the constable appeared, carrying a breakfast tray. He was whistling cheerfully. He came up to the barred door of her cell and looked in. And his whistling died on his lips as if it had run down and needed to be wound up again. But this comical astonishment lasted for a moment only. And then his face flushed red with anger.

Winnie had sat on the cot, eyes downcast, feeling very small—and very like a criminal. In fact, he was soon shouting that if she were older, he'd have to keep her there—that it *was* a crime, what she had done. She was . . . an accomplice. She had helped a murderer escape. She was, in fact, a criminal. But too young to be punished by the law. Worse luck, he told her, for she badly needed punishing.

She was released, then, into the custody of her mother and father. And these new words, "accomplice" and "custody," chilled her blood. Over and over they asked her, shocked at first and then wistful:

why had she *done* such a thing? *Why?* She was their daughter. They had trusted her. They had tried to bring her up properly, with a true sense of right and wrong. They did not understand. And finally she had sobbed the only truth there was into her mother's shoulder, the only explanation: the Tucks were her friends. She had done it because—in spite of everything, she loved them.

This of all things her family understood, and afterward they drew together staunchly around her. It was hard for them in the village, Winnie knew it was, and the knowledge gave her pain. For they were proud. And she had shamed them. Still, this side of the affair was not without its benefits, at least for Winnie. Though she was confined to the yard indefinitely and could go nowhere, not even with her mother or her grandmother, the other children wandered by to look at her, to talk to her through the fence. They were impressed by what she had done. She was a figure of romance to them now, where before she had been too neat, too prissy; almost, somehow, too *clean* to be a real friend.

Winnie sighed and plucked at the grass around her ankles. School would open soon. It wouldn't be so bad. In fact, she thought as her spirits lifted, this year it might be rather nice.

And then two things happened. First of all, the toad appeared out of the weeds, on her side of the road this time. It bounced out of a cover of old dandelion leaves and landed—plop!—just beyond the fence. If she had reached her hand through the bars, she could have touched it. And next, a large brown dog, with easy gait and dangling tongue, came loping down the road toward them. He stopped opposite the fence and looked at Winnie with a friendly swish of his tail, and then he saw the toad. At once he began to bark, his eyes bright. He pranced up, his hind quarters leaping independently from side to side, nose close to the toad, his voice shrill with enthusiasm.

"Don't!" cried Winnie, leaping to her feet and flapping her arms. "Go away, dog! Stop that! Go away—shoo!"

The dog paused. He looked up at Winnie's frantic dancing and then he looked at the toad, who had pressed down close to the dirt, eyes tight shut. It was too much for him. He began to bark again, and reached out a long paw.

"Oh!" cried Winnie. "Oh—*don't* do that! Leave my toad *alone!*" And before she had time to realize what she was doing, she bent, reached through the bars, and snatched the toad up and away from harm, dropping it on the grass inside the fence.

A feeling of revulsion swept through her. While the dog whined, pawing uselessly at the fence, she stood rigid, staring at the toad, wiping her hand again and again on the skirt of her dress. Then she remembered the actual feel of the toad, and the revulsion passed. She knelt and touched the skin of its back. It was rough and soft, both at once. And cool.

Winnie stood up and looked at the dog. He was waiting outside the fence, his head on one side, peering at her longingly. "It's *my* toad," Winnie told him. "So you'd better leave it alone." And then, on an impulse, she turned and ran into the cottage, up to her room, to the bureau drawer where she had hidden Jesse's bottle—the bottle of water from the spring. In a moment she was back again. The toad still squatted where she had dropped it, the dog still waited at the fence. Winnie pulled out the cork from the mouth of the bottle, and kneeling, she poured the precious water, very slowly and carefully, over the toad.

The dog watched this operation, and then, yawning, he was suddenly bored. He turned and loped away, back down the road to the village. Winnie picked up the toad and held it for a long time, without the least disgust, in the palm of her hand. It sat calmly, blinking, and the water glistened on its back.

The little bottle was empty now. It lay on the grass at Winnie's feet. But if all of it was true, there was more water in the wood. There was plenty more. Just in case. When she was seventeen. If she should decide, there was more water in the wood. Winnie smiled. Then she stooped and put her hand through the fence and set the toad free. "There!" she said. "You're safe. Forever."

Epilogue

The sign said WELCOME TO TREEGAP, but it was hard to believe that this was really Treegap. The main street hadn't changed so very much, but there were many other streets now, crossing the main street. The road itself was blacktopped. There was a white line painted down its center.

Mae and Tuck, on the seat of a clattering wooden wagon, bumped slowly into Treegap behind the fat old horse. They had seen continuous change and were accustomed to it, but here it seemed shocking and sad. "Look," said Tuck. "Look, Mae. Ain't that where the wood used to be? It's gone! Not a stick or a stump left! And her cottage—that's gone, too."

It was very hard to recognize anything, but from the little hill, which had once lain outside the village and was now very much a part of it, they thought they could figure things out. "Yes," said Mae, "that's where it was, I do believe. 'Course, it's been so long since we was here, I can't tell for certain."

There was a gas station there now. A young man in greasy coveralls was polishing the windshield of a wide and rusty Hudson automobile. As Mae and Tuck rolled past, the young man grinned and said to the driver of the Hudson, who lounged at the wheel, "Looky there. In from the country for a big time." And they chuckled together.

Mae and Tuck clattered on into the village proper, past a catholic mixture of houses which soon gave way to shops and other places of business: a hot-dog stand; a dry cleaner; a pharmacy; a five-and-ten; another gas station; a tall, white frame building with a pleasant verandah, The Treegap Hotel—Family Dining, Easy Rates. The post office. Beyond that, the jailhouse, but a larger jailhouse now, painted brown, with an office for the county clerk. A black and white police car was parked in front, with a red glass searchlight on its roof and a radio antenna, like a buggy whip, fastened to the windshield.

Mae glanced at the jailhouse, but looked away quickly. "See beyond there?" she said, pointing. "That diner? Let's stop there and get a cup of coffee. All right?"

"All right," said Tuck. "Maybe they'll know something."

Inside, the diner gleamed with chrome and smelled like linoleum and ketchup. Mae and Tuck took seats on rumbling swivel stools at the long counter. The counterman emerged from the kitchen at the rear and sized them up expertly. They looked all right. A little queer, maybe—their clothes, especially—but honest. He slapped a cardboard menu down in front of them and leaned on the foaming orangeade cooler. "You folks from off?" he asked.

"Yep," said Tuck. "Just passing through."

"Sure," said the counterman.

"Say," said Tuck cautiously, fingering the menu. "Didn't there used to be a wood once, down the other side of town?"

"Sure," said the counterman. "Had a big electrical storm, though, about three years ago now or thereabouts. Big tree got hit by lightning, split right down the middle. Caught fire and everything. Tore up the ground, too. Had to bulldoze her all out."

"Oh," said Tuck. He and Mae exchanged glances.

"Coffee, please," said Mae. "Black. For both of us."

"Sure," said the counterman. He took the menu away, poured coffee into thick pottery mugs, and leaned again on the orangeade cooler.

"Used to be a fresh-water spring in that wood," said Tuck boldly, sipping his coffee.

"Don't know nothing about that," said the counterman. "Had to bulldoze her all out, like I say."

"Oh," said Tuck.

Afterward, while Mae was shopping for supplies, Tuck went back through the town on foot—back the way they had come—out to the little hill. There were houses there now, and a feed-and-grain store, but on the far side of the hill, inside a rambling iron fence, was a cemetery.

Tuck's heart quickened. He had noticed the cemetery on the way in. Mae had seen it, too. They had not spoken about it. But both knew it might hold other answers. Tuck straightened his old jacket. He passed through an archway of wrought-iron curlicues, and paused, squinting at the weedy rows of gravestones. And then, far over to the right, he saw a tall monument, once no doubt imposing but now tipped slightly sidewise. On it was carved one name: Foster.

Slowly, Tuck turned his footsteps toward the monument. And saw, as he approached, that there were other, smaller markers all around it. A family plot. And then his throat closed. For it was there. He had wanted it to be there, but now that he saw it, he was overcome with sadness. He knelt and read the inscription:

In Loving Memory
Winifred Foster Jackson
Dear Wife
Dear Mother
1870–1948

"So," said Tuck to himself. "Two years. She's been gone two years." He stood up and looked around, embarrassed, trying to clear the lump from his throat. But there was no one to see him. The cemetery was very quiet. In the branches of a willow behind him, a red-winged blackbird chirped. Tuck wiped his eyes hastily. Then he straightened his jacket again and drew up his hand in a brief salute. "Good girl," he said aloud. And then he turned and left the cemetery, walking quickly.

Later, as he and Mae rolled out of Treegap, Mae said softly, without looking at him, "She's gone?"

Tuck nodded. "She's gone," he answered.

There was a long moment of silence between them, and then Mae said, "Poor Jesse."

"He knowed it, though," said Tuck. "At least, he knowed she wasn't coming. We all knowed that, long time ago."

"Just the same," said Mae. She sighed. And then she sat up a little straighter. "Well, where to now, Tuck? No need to come back here no more."

"That's so," said Tuck. "Let's just head on out this way. We'll locate something."

"All right," said Mae. And then she put a hand on his arm and pointed. "Look out for that toad."

Tuck had seen it, too. He reined in the horse and climbed down from the wagon. The toad was squatting in the middle of the road, quite unconcerned. In the other lane, a pickup truck rattled by, and against the breeze it made, the toad shut its eyes tightly. But it did not move. Tuck waited till the truck had passed, and then he picked up the toad and carried it to the weeds along the road's edge. "Durn fool thing must think it's going to live forever," he said to Mae.

And soon they were rolling on again, leaving Treegap behind, and as they went, the tinkling little melody of a music box drifted out behind them and was lost at last far down the road.

CONNECTIONS

"I don't want to die," Winnie complains. Each of these American Indian myths presents a very different explanation of how the universe works and why people must die. Think about whether Angus Tuck would agree or disagree with these descriptions of the natural order of things—and whether you do.

Coyote and the Origin of Death
a Caddo myth

from American Indian Myths and Legends recorded by Richard Erdoes

In the beginning of this world, there was no such thing as death. Everybody continued to live until there were so many people that the earth had no room for any more. The chiefs held a council to determine what to do. One man rose and said he thought it would be a good plan to have the people die and be gone for a little while, and then return.

As soon as he sat down, Coyote jumped up and said he thought people ought to die forever. He pointed out that this little world is not large enough to hold all of the people, and that if the people who died came back to life, there would not be food enough for all.

All the other men objected. They said that they did not want their friends and relatives to die and be gone forever, for then they would grieve and worry and there would be no happiness in the world. Everyone except Coyote decided to have people die and be gone for a little while, and then come back to life again.

The medicine men built a large grass house facing the

east. When they had completed it, they called the men of the tribe together and told them that people who died would be restored to life in the medicine house. The chief medicine man explained that they would sing a song calling the spirit of the dead to the grass house. When the spirit came, they would restore it to life. All the people were glad, because they were anxious for the dead to come and live with them again.

When the first man died, the medicine men assembled in the grass house and sang. In about ten days a whirlwind blew from the west and circled about the grass house. Coyote saw it, and as the whirlwind was about the enter the house, he closed the door. The spirit of the whirlwind, finding the door closed, whirled on by. In this way Coyote made death eternal, and from that time on, people grieved over their dead and were unhappy.

Now whenever anyone meets a whirlwind or hears the wind whistle, he says: "Someone is wandering about." Ever since Coyote closed the door, the spirits of the dead have wandered over the earth trying to find some place to go, until at last they discovered the road to the spirit land.

Coyote ran away and never came back, for when he saw what he had done, he was afraid. Ever after that, he has run from one place to another, always looking back first over one shoulder and then over the other to see if anyone is pursuing him. And ever since then he has been starving, for no one will give him anything to eat.

—*From a tale reported by George A. Dorsey in 1905*

The End of the World

a Sioux myth

told by Jenny Leading Cloud
from American Indian Myths and Legends
recorded by Richard Erdoes

Somewhere at a place where the prairie and the Maka Sicha, the Badlands, meet, there is a hidden cave. Not for a long, long time has anyone been able to find it. Even now, with so many highways, cars, and tourists, no one has discovered this cave.

In it lives a woman so old that her face looks like a shriveled-up walnut. She is dressed in rawhide, the way people used to be before the white man came. She has been sitting there for a thousand years or more, working on a blanket strip for her buffalo robe. She is making the strip out of dyed porcupine quills, the way our ancestors did before white traders brought glass beads to this turtle continent. Resting beside her, licking his paws, watching her all the time is Shunka Sapa, a huge black dog. His eyes never wander from the old woman, whose teeth are worn flat, worn down to little stumps, she has used them to flatten so many porcupine quills.

A few steps from where the old woman sits working on her blanket strip, a huge fire is kept going. She lit this fire a thousand or more years ago and has kept it alive ever since. Over the fire hangs a big earthen pot, the kind some Indian peoples used to make before the white man came with his kettles of iron. Inside the big pot, *wojapi* is boiling and bubbling. *Wojapi* is berry soup, good and sweet and red. That soup has been boiling in the pot for a long time, ever since the fire was lit.

Every now and then the old woman gets up to stir the

wojapi in the huge earthen pot. She is so old and feeble that it takes her a while to get up and hobble over to the fire. The moment her back is turned, the huge black dog starts pulling the porcupine quills out of her blanket strip. This way she never makes any progress, and her quillwork remains forever unfinished. The Sioux people used to say that if the old woman ever finishes her blanket strip, then at the very moment that she threads the last porcupine quill to complete the design, the world will come to an end.

It Is Better to Die Forever

a Blackfoot myth
retold by Chewing Blackbones

from Indian Legends from the Northern Rockies

collected by Ella E. Clark

Long, long ago, there were only two persons in the world: Old Man and Old Woman. One time when they were traveling about the earth, Old Woman said to Old Man, "Now let us come to an agreement of some kind. Let us decide how the people shall live when they shall be on the earth."

"Well," replied Old Man, "I am to have the first say in everything."

"I agree with you," said Old Woman. "That is—if I may have the second say."

Then Old Man began his plans. "The women will have the duty of tanning the hides. They will rub animals' brains on the hides to make them soft and scrape them with scraping tools. All this they will do very quickly, for it will not be hard work."

"No," said Old Woman, "I will not agree to this. They must tan hides in the way you say; but it must be very hard work, so that the good workers may be found out."

"Well," said Old Man, "We will let the people have eyes and mouths, straight up and down in their faces."

"No," replied Old Woman, "let us not have them that way. We will have the eyes and mouths in the faces, as you say, but they shall be set crosswise."

"Well," said Old Man, "the people shall have ten fingers on each hand."

"Oh, no!" replied Old Woman. "That will be too many. They will be in the way. There will be four fingers and one thumb on each hand."

So the two went on until they had provided for everything in the lives of the people who were to be.

"What shall we do about life and death?" asked Old Woman. "Should the people live forever, or should they die?"

Old Woman and Old Man had difficulty agreeing about this. Finally Old Man said, "I will tell you what we will do. I will throw a buffalo chip into the water. If it floats, the people will die for four days and then come to life again; if it sinks, they will die forever."

So he threw a buffalo chip into the water, and it floated.

"No," said Old Woman, "we will not decide in that way. I will throw this rock into the water. If it floats, the people will die for four days; if it sinks, they will die forever."

Then Old Woman threw the rock into the water, and it sank to the bottom.

"There," said she. "It is better for the people to die forever. If they did not, they would not feel sorry for each other, and there would be no sympathy in the world."

"Well," said Old Man, "let it be that way."

After a time, Old Woman had a daughter, who soon became sick and died. The mother was very sorry then that they had agreed that people should die forever. "Let us have our say over again," she said.

"No," replied Old Man. "Let us not change what we have agreed upon."

And so people have died ever since.

■ ■ ■

Eternal youth—everyone seems to want it, but what would it really be like? This story presents a vision of everlasting youth that you might not find very appealing. Would many people choose eternal youth if this is what it was like?

Hail and Farewell
Ray Bradbury

But of course he was going away, there was nothing else to do, the time was up, the clock had run out, and he was going very far away indeed. His suitcase was packed, his shoes were shined, his hair was brushed, he had expressly washed behind his ears, and it remained only for him to go down the stairs, out the front door, and up the street to the small-town station where the train would make a stop for him alone. Then Fox Hill, Illinois, would be left far off in his past. And he would go on, perhaps to Iowa, perhaps to Kansas, perhaps even to California; a small boy twelve years old with a birth certificate in his valise to show he had been born forty-three years ago.

"Willie!" called a voice downstairs.

"Yes!" He hoisted his suitcase. In his bureau mirror he saw a face made of June dandelions and July apples and warm summer-morning milk. There, as always, was his look of the angel and the innocent, which might never, in the years of his life, change.

"Almost time," called the woman's voice.

"All right!" And he went down the stairs, grunting and smiling. In the living room sat Anna and Steve, their clothes painfully neat.

"Here I am!" cried Willie in the parlor door.

Anna looked like she was going to cry. "Oh good Lord, you can't really be leaving us, can you, Willie?"

"People are beginning to talk," said Willie quietly. "I've been here three years now. But when people begin to talk, I know it's time to put on my shoes and buy a railway ticket."

"It's all so strange. I don't understand. It's so sudden," Anna said. "Willie, we'll miss you."

"I'll write you every Christmas, so help me. Don't you write me."

"It's been a great pleasure and satisfaction," said Steve, sitting there, his words the wrong size in his mouth. "It's a shame it had to stop. It's a shame you had to tell us about yourself. It's an awful shame you can't stay on."

"You're the nicest folks I ever had," said Willie, four feet high, in no need of a shave, the sunlight on his face.

And then Anna *did* cry. "Willie, Willie." And she sat down and looked as if she wanted to hold him but was afraid to hold him now; she looked at him with shock and amazement and her hands empty, not knowing what to do with him now.

"It's not easy to go," said Willie. "You get used to things. You want to stay. But it doesn't work. I tried to stay on once after people began to suspect. 'How horrible!' people said. 'All these years, playing with our innocent children,' they said, 'and us not guessing! Awful!' they said. And finally I had to just leave town one night. It's not easy. You know darned well how much I love both of you. Thanks for three swell years."

They all went to the front door. "Willie, where're you going?"

"I don't know. I just start traveling. When I see a town

that looks green and nice, I settle in."

"Will you ever come back?"

"Yes," he said earnestly with his high voice. "In about twenty years it should begin to show in my face. When it does, I'm going to make a grand tour of all the mothers and fathers I've ever had."

They stood on the cool summer porch, reluctant to say the last words. Steve was looking steadily at an elm tree. "How many other folks've you stayed with, Willie? How many adoptions?"

Willie figured it, pleasantly enough. "I guess it's about five towns and five couples and over twenty years gone by since I started my tour."

"Well, we can't holler," said Steve. "Better to've had a son thirty-six months than none whatever."

"Well," said Willie, and kissed Anna quickly, seized at his luggage, and was gone up the street in the green noon light, under the trees, a very young boy indeed, not looking back, running steadily.

The boys were playing on the green park diamond when he came by. He stood a little while among the oak-tree shadows, watching them hurl the white, snowy baseball into the warm summer air, saw the baseball shadow fly like a dark bird over the grass, saw their hands open in mouths to catch this swift piece of summer that now seemed most especially important to hold on to. The boys' voices yelled. The ball lit on the grass near Willie.

Carrying the ball forward from under the shade trees, he thought of the last three years now spent to the penny, and the five years before that, and so on down the line to the year when he was really eleven and twelve and fourteen and the voices saying: "What's wrong with Willie, missus?" "Mrs. B., is Willie late a-growin'?" "Willie, you smokin' cigars lately?" The echoes died in summer light and color. His mother's voice: "Willie's twenty-one today!" And a thousand voices saying: "Come back, son, when you're fifteen; *then* maybe we'll give you a job."

He stared at the baseball in his trembling hand, as if it were his life, an interminable ball of years strung around and around and around, but always leading back to his twelfth birthday. He heard the kids walking toward him; he felt them blot out the sun, and they were older, standing around him.

"Willie! Where you goin'?" They kicked his suitcase.

How tall they stood in the sun. In the last few months it seemed the sun had passed a hand above their heads, beckoned, and they were warm metal drawn melting upward; they were golden taffy pulled by an immense gravity to the sky, thirteen, fourteen years old, looking down upon Willie, smiling, but already beginning to neglect him. It had started four months ago:

"Choose up sides! Who wants Willie?"

"Aw, Willie's too little; we don't play with 'kids.'"

And they raced ahead of him, drawn by the moon and the sun and the turning seasons of leaf and wind, and he was twelve years old and not of them any more. And the other voices beginning again on the old, the dreadfully familiar, the cool refrain: "Better feed that boy vitamins, Steve." "Anna, does shortness *run* in your family?" And the cold fist knocking at your heart again and knowing that the roots would have to be pulled up again after so many good years with the "folks."

"Willie, where you goin'?"

He jerked his head. He was back among the towering, shadowing boys who milled around him like giants at a drinking fountain bending down.

"Goin' a few days visitin' a cousin of mine."

"Oh." There was a day, a year ago, when they would have cared very much indeed. But now there was only curiosity for his luggage, their enchantment with trains and trips and far places.

"How about a coupla fast ones?" said Willie.

They looked doubtful, but, considering the circumstances, nodded. He dropped his bag and ran out; the white baseball was up in the sun, away to their burning white figures in the far meadow, up in the sun again, rushing, life coming and going in a pattern. Here, *there!* Mr. and Mrs. Robert Hanlon, Creek Bend, Wisconsin, 1932, the first couple, the first year! Here, *there!* Henry and Alice Boltz, Limeville, Iowa, 1935! The baseball flying. The Smiths, the Eatons, the Robinsons! 1939! 1945! Husband and wife, husband and wife, husband and wife, no children, no children! A knock on this door, a knock on that.

"Pardon me. My name is William. I wonder if—"

"A sandwich? Come in, sit down. Where you *from,* son?"

The sandwich, a tall glass of cold milk, the smiling, the nodding, the comfortable leisurely talking.

"Son, you look like you been traveling. You run *off* from somewhere?"

"No."

"Boy, are you an orphan?"

Another glass of milk.

"We always wanted kids. It never worked out. Never knew why. One of those things. Well, well. It's getting late, son. Don't you think you better hit for home?"

"Got no home."

"A boy like you? Not dry behind the ears? Your mother'll be worried."

"Got no home and no folks anywhere in the world. I wonder if—I wonder—could I sleep here tonight?"

"Well, now, son, I don't just know. We never considered taking in—" said the husband.

"We got chicken for supper tonight," said the wife, "enough for extras, enough for company. . . ."

And the years turning and flying away, the voices, and the faces, and the people, and always the same first conversations. The voice of Emily Robinson, in her rocking chair, in summer-night darkness, the last night he stayed with her, the night she discovered his secret, her voice saying:

"I look at all the little children's faces going by. And I sometimes think, What a shame, what a shame, that all these flowers have to be cut, all these bright fires have to be put out. What a shame these, all of these you see in schools or running by, have to get tall and unsightly and wrinkle and turn gray or get bald, and finally, all bone and wheeze, be dead and buried off away. When I hear them laugh I can't believe they'll ever go the road I'm going. Yet here they *come!* I still remember Wordsworth's poem: 'When all at once I saw a crowd, A host of golden daffodils; Beside the lake, beneath the trees, Fluttering and dancing in the breeze.' That's how I think of children, cruel as they sometimes are, mean as I know they can be, but not yet showing the meanness around their eyes or *in* their eyes, not yet full of tiredness. They're so eager for everything! I guess that's what I miss most in older folks, the eagerness gone nine times out of ten, the freshness gone, so much of the drive and life down the drain. I like to watch school let out each

day. It's like someone threw a bunch of flowers out the
school front doors. How does it feel, Willie? How does it feel
to be young forever? To look like a silver dime new from
the mint? Are you happy? Are you as fine as you *seem?*"

The baseball whizzed from the blue sky, stung his hand
like a great pale insect. Nursing it, he hears his memory say:

"I worked with what I had. After my folks died, after I
found I couldn't get man's work anywhere, I tried carnivals,
but they only laughed. 'Son,' they said 'you're not a midget,
and even if you are, you look like a *boy!* We want midgets
with midgets' *faces!* Sorry, son, sorry.' So I left home, started
out, thinking: What *was* I? A boy. I looked like a boy,
sounded like a boy, so I might as well go on being a boy.
No use fighting it. No use screaming. So what could I do?
What job was handy? And then one day I saw this man in a
restaurant looking at another man's pictures of his children.
'Sure wish I had kids,' he said. 'Sure wish I had kids.' He
kept shaking his head. And me sitting a few seats away from
him, a hamburger in my hands. I sat there, *frozen!* At that
very instant I knew what my job would be for all the rest of
my life. There *was* work for me, after all. Making lonely
people happy. Keeping myself busy. Playing forever. I knew
I had to play forever. Deliver a few papers, run a few
errands, mow a few lawns, maybe. But *hard* work? No. All I
had to do was be a mother's son and a father's pride. I
turned to the man down the counter from me. 'I beg your
pardon,' I said. I *smiled* at him. . . ."

"But, Willie," said Mrs. Emily long ago, "didn't you ever
get lonely? Didn't you ever want—*things*—that grown-ups
wanted?"

"I fought that out alone," said Willie. "I'm a boy, I told

myself, I'll have to live in a boy's world, read boys' books, play boys' games, cut myself off from everything else. I can't be both. I got to be only one thing—young. And so I played that way. Oh, it wasn't easy. There were times—" He lapsed into silence.

"And the family you lived with, they never knew?"

"No. Telling them would have spoiled everything. I told them I was a runaway; I let them check through official channels, police. Then, when there was no record, let them put in to adopt me. That was best of all; as long as they never guessed. But then, after three years, or five years, they guessed, or a traveling man came through, or a carnival man saw me, and it was over. It always had to end."

"And you're very happy and it's nice being a child for over forty years?"

"It's a living, as they say. And when you make other people happy, then you're almost happy too. I got my job to do and I do it. And anyway, in a few years now I'll be in my second childhood. All the fevers will be out of me and all the unfulfilled things and most of the dreams. Then I can relax, maybe, and play the role all the way."

He threw the baseball one last time and broke the reverie. Then he was running to seize his luggage. Tom, Bill, Jamie, Bob, Sam—their names moved on his lips. They were embarrassed at his shaking hands.

"After all, Willie, it ain't as if you're going to China or Timbuktu."

"That's right, isn't it?" Willie did not move.

"So long, Willie. See you next week!"

"So long, so long!"

And he was walking off with his suitcase again, looking at the trees, going away from the boys and the street where he had lived, and as he turned the corner a train whistle screamed, and he began to run.

The last thing he saw and heard was a white ball tossed at a high roof, back and forth, back and forth, and two voices crying out as the ball pitched now up, down, and back through the sky, "Annie, annie, over! Annie, annie, over!" like the crying of birds flying off to the far south.

In the early morning, with the smell of the mist and the cold metal, with the iron smell of the train around him and a full night of traveling shaking his bones and his body, and a smell of the sun beyond the horizon, he awoke and looked out upon a small town just arising from sleep. Lights were coming on, soft voices muttered, a red signal bobbed back and forth, back and forth in the cold air. There was that sleeping hush in which echoes are dignified by clarity, in which echoes stand nakedly alone and sharp. A porter moved by, a shadow in shadows.

"Sir," said Willie.

The porter stopped.

"What town's this?" whispered the boy in the dark.

"Valleyville."

"How many people?"

"Ten thousand. Why? This your stop?"

"It looks green." Willie gazed out at the cold morning town for a long time. "It looks nice and quiet," said Willie.

"Son," said the porter "you know where you *going?*"

"Here," said Willie, and got up quietly in the still, cool, iron-smelling morning, in the train dark, with a rustling and stir.

"I hope you know what you're doing, boy," said the porter.

"Yes, sir," said Willie. "I know what I'm doing." And he was down the dark aisle, luggage lifted after him by the porter, and out in the smoking, steaming-cold, beginning-to-lighten morning. He stood looking up at the porter and the black metal train against the few remaining stars. The train gave a great wailing blast of whistle, the porters cried out all along the line, the cars jolted, and his special porter waved and smiled down at the boy there, the small boy there with the big luggage who shouted up to him, even as the whistle screamed again.

"What?" shouted the porter, hand cupped to ear.

"Wish me luck!" cried Willie.

"Best of luck, son," called the porter, waving, smiling. "Best of luck, boy!"

"Thanks," said Willie, in the great sound of the train, in the steam and roar.

He watched the black train until it was completely gone away and out of sight. He did not move all the time it was going. He stood quietly, a small boy twelve years old, on the worn wooden platform, and only after three entire minutes did he turn at last to face the empty streets below.

Then, as the sun was rising, he began to walk very fast, so as to keep warm, down into the new town.

■ ■ ■

By the end of Tuck Everlasting, *Winnie Foster probably feels
that she's had a crash course in immortality. Peter Robinson has
a lot to learn about immortality at the beginning of this story. Do
you think there is anything Winnie could tell Peter to save him
some trouble?*

How to Live Forever
Colin Thompson

In a quiet street of tall trees there is a library with a thousand
rooms. On the shelves are copies of every book that has ever
been written.

But one book is missing. Two hundred years ago someone hid
its record card under the bottom drawer of a filing cabinet,
and the book quietly vanished.

The book is called *How to Live Forever.*

When the library is closed and the night watchman has fallen
asleep in his big armchair, the shelves come to life. Doors
and windows appear on the backs of the books, lights come
on, and the sound of voices drifts out between the pages.
Full-grown trees spring up and chimneys begin to smoke.
Staircases and ladders join the shelves into great cities, and in
the distance small dogs bark.

On a shelf of cookbooks beginning with the letter *Q*, in a book
called *Quinces,* lived a family named Robinson; a mother, a
father, a serious girl named Lucy and a boy named Peter.

Peter was the only person who knew about the missing book. One night his cat, Brian, chased a mouse into the filing cabinet, and when Peter squeezed in after him, he found the card. When he went to get the book, there was only a dark, dust-filled gap. Peter decided that no matter what he had to do, he would find the lost book.

"If I can find it," he said to Brian, "we will never grow old."

Every night for the next two years Peter and Brian searched for the book.

On the shelves near the empty space there were books about age-old medicines and health books full of exercises and salads. Peter walked past rows of books with people in leotards leaping about, eating celery, and having their thighs photographed. But it was always the same. When he looked closely, they all had wrinkles around their eyes. They were getting older. *They* didn't know about the book.

"Where's that boy off to every night?" said his mother.

"As long as he's not getting into any trouble, it's all right," said his father.

Peter traveled from room to room, through secret cellars of forbidden books to well-worn shelves of cowboy stories, through silent books of Braille to the street guides of lost cities.

And then, on a dark shelf below the ceiling in a long-forgotten attic, Peter found four old men standing ankle-deep in dust, each balanced on one leg in front of a row of ancient Chinese books. The old men had white hair and deeply lined faces. *They* surely didn't know about the book. Peter watched them. If it hadn't been for their gentle breathing, the old men could have been statues.

"Welcome," said the first old man. He put his foot down very slowly, so as not to disturb the dust, and bowed.

"You are just in time for tea," said the second. He too put his foot on the ground and bowed. The third man did the same. The fourth man didn't move, and when Peter looked closer, he saw that he was asleep.

"We don't get many visitors," said the first old man.

"You're the first," said the second.

Peter followed the old men into a large faded book. It was filled with the scent of spices and ancient memories. Beautiful carpets covered the floors, and red-lacquered shelves crammed with a thousand treasures filled the walls.

"You've come for this, haven't you?" said the third man, holding out a small book.

Peter took it and read the faded words:

How to Live Forever, or *Immortality for Beginners.*

Peter couldn't understand it. If these four old men had the book, why were they so old? He thought for a moment.

"It doesn't work, does it?" he said.

"Oh, yes, it works," said one of the old men.

"Well, why . . ." began Peter.

"Why are we so old?"

"Yes."

"Follow me," said the old man, "and I will show you."

He led Peter through a door into a Chinese garden. It was the most beautiful place the boy had ever seen. Delicate trees shivered in a soft breeze. Their blossoms fell into pools of clear water filled with silent fish. Chinese quail picked across the earth, and bright butterflies flew around his head. Peter just wanted to stand and stare, but the old man was walking off down the path.

"Where are we going?" said Peter, running after him.

"To see the Ancient Child," said the old man.

Peter followed the old man through the trees into a clearing. There, in a large chair, sat the Ancient Child. He was both young and old, ten and timeless at the same time. His skin was as smooth as a child's, but it was dull and tired. His eyes were a child's eyes, but they were weary and far away.

"This young one has come for the book," said the old man.

"You mustn't read it," said the Ancient Child. "It will drive you mad."

"I am the only person," he went on, "who has read it and not lost his mind. I was younger than you when I found it, and I couldn't read it fast enough. Then, while my friends grew up, I stayed like this. They grew out of toys and fell in love. They married and had children, and all I could do was sit and watch. Now I am frozen in time. I keep saying that I had everything, but all I had was endless tomorrows. To live forever is to not live at all. That's why I hid the book."

"Why didn't you just burn it?" asked Peter.

"The book is immortal, too," said the Ancient Child.

Peter walked through the garden feeling quite desolate. When he reached the pool, he sat down on the warm earth. All afternoon he watched the goldfish. They too were growing old, but their children were swimming in their shadows.

"I won't read it," he said, and went back to the Ancient Child.

"You are wiser than I was," said the Ancient Child, and led him back to the world.

■ ■ ■

The Tucks never intended to live forever; they were just stopping for a drink of water when they stumbled into immortality. In this Irish legend, a heroic figure loses hundreds of years when he travels to a faraway land. Might he reconsider his actions if he knew the consequences?

The Return of Oisin
an Irish legend
retold by Rosemary Sutcliff

In the Valley of the Thrushes, not far from where Dublin stands today, a crowd of men were trying to shift a great boulder from their tilled land, the village headman directing their efforts. The stone had been there as long as any of them could remember, or their grandfathers before them, and always they had grumbled at it because it got in the way of the plowing. But though one or two half-hearted attempts had been made to shift it, it still lay half embedded in the hillside, where it always had lain.

Now at last, they were really set upon getting rid of the thing, and every man in the village had gathered to lend his strength to the task.

But it seemed that their strength was all too little, for there they were heaving and straining and grunting and hauling, their faces crimson and the sweat running off them, and the great boulder not moving so much as a finger's breadth out of its bed.

And as they strained and struggled—and they getting nearer each moment to giving up—they saw riding toward them a horseman such as none of them had ever set eyes on before, save maybe in some glorious dream. Taller and mightier than any man of this world he was, and riding a foam-white stallion as far beyond mortal horses as he was beyond mortal men. His eyes were strangely dark, his fair hair like a sunburst about his head. A mantle of saffron silk flowed back from brooches of yellow gold that clasped it at his shoulders, and at his side hung a great golden-hilted sword.

"It is one of the Fairy Kind!" said an aged villager, making the sign of the horns with the two first fingers of his left hand.

"It is an archangel out of Heaven!" said a young one, and made the sign of the Cross.

The splendid being, man or fairy or angel, reined in his horse, and sat looking down at them with a puzzled pity on his face. "You wanted this shifting?" he said.

The headman drew nearer, greatly daring. "We did so, but it seems 'tis beyond our strength. Would you be lending us the power of your arm, now?"

"Surely," said the rider, and stooping from the saddle, set his hand under the boulder and gave a mighty heave. The boulder came out of the ground and went rolling over and over down the hillside like a shinty ball, and the watching villagers gave a great shout of wonder and admiration. But next moment their shouts turned to fearful and wondering dismay.

For as he heaved at the boulder, the rider's saddle girth had burst, so that he fell headlong to the ground. The moment the white stallion felt himself free, he neighed three times and set off at a tearing gallop toward the coast, and as he went, he seemed not merely to grow small with distance, but to lose shape and substance and fade into the summer air like a wisp of woodsmoke.

And there on the ground, where the splendid stranger had fallen, lay an old, old man, huge still, but with thin white beard and milky half-blind eyes, his silken mantle a patched and tattered cloak of coarsest homespun, his golden-hilted sword a rough ash stick such as a blind old beggar might use to support him and feel his way about the world. He half raised himself and peered about, then with a wild despairing cry, stretched all his length again burying his head in his arms.

In a little, seeing that nothing terrible seemed to have happened to any of themselves, some of the bolder of the villagers came closer and lifted him up and asked him who he was.

"I am Oisin the son of Finn Mac Cool," said the old man.

Then the villagers looked at each other, and the headman said, "If you mean who I think you mean, then you're as crazy as we must have been just now to be taking you for whatever it was we took you for."

"It was the sun in our eyes," said another man.

And they asked the old man a second time who he was.

"Why do you ask again, when I have already told you? I am Oisin the son of Finn Mac Cool, Captain of the Fianna of Erin."

"It is the sun on that bald head of yours," said the headman, kindly enough. "Finn Mac Cool and his heroes we have heard of, yes, but they have been dead these three hundred years."

Then the old man was silent a long while, his face bowed into his hands. At last he said, "How did they die?"

"At the Battle of Gavra, not so far from here at all. There is a green mound up there beside the battleground. I was hearing once it was the grave of one of them, called Osca. A great battle it was, and they do say that there were none but boys and old men left in Erin when the fighting was done."

"But Oisin did not die then," another put in. "No man knows the death of Oisin, but the harpers still sing the songs he made."

"But now Priest Patrick has come into Erin, and told us of the one true God, and Christ His Son, and the old days are done with, and we listen to them only as men listen to old tales that are half forgotten."

The old man seemed half-dazed, like one that has taken a blow between the eyes. Only he cried out once, harshly and near to choking, "Strong and without mercy is your new God! And He has much to answer for if He has slain the memory of Finn and Osca!"

Then the people were angry and cried "Sacrilege!" and some of them picked up the small surface stones of the field to throw at the old man. But the headman bade them let him be until Priest Patrick had seen him and told them what they should do.

So they took him to the old fortress of Drum Derg, where Patrick had at that time made his living place.

And Patrick listened to their account of how he had come to them, and how, with the sun in their eyes they had mistaken him for a young man and asked his aid in moving the great stone from their tilled land, and of what had happened after.

And Patrick was kind to the huge half-blind old beggar, and gave him a place for sleeping and a place for sitting by the fire, among his own Christian brotherhood.

And often the priest of the new God, and the old man who had been Oisin would talk together. And Oisin told wonderful stories of Finn and the Fianna and the High and Far-off Days, which Patrick bade one of his scribes to write down on pages of fair white sheepskin, lest they should be forgotten.

As time went by, Patrick came to believe that the old man was indeed Oisin the son of Finn Mac Cool, and one day he said to him, "It is upward of three hundred years since Finn and Osca and the flower of the Fianna died at Gavra. Tell me then, how is it that you have lived so long beyond your day and the days of your companions?"

So Oisin told him this last story: the story of how he had ridden hunting with the Fianna one summer morning among the lakes of Killarney, and how the Princess Niamh of the Golden

Hair had come out of the West, and asked him to return to
Tyr-na-nOg with her. And how he had taken leave of Finn and
Osca and the rest, and mounted behind her on her white horse,
and how they had headed westward again until they came to the
sea, and headed westward still, leaving the companions of the
Fianna behind them on the shore.

And when he reached that point in his story, Oisin buried his
face in his hands and seemed to forget.

Then, to rouse him, and because he was a man of curiosity
and interest in all things, Patrick said, "Success and benediction!
Tell me what happened after that."

And Oisin raised his head again, and staring with half-blind
eyes into the heart of the fire, as though he saw there all things
happening again, he went on with his story.

"The white horse galloped across the waves as lightly as he
had done across the green hills of Erin, and the wind overtook
the waves, and we overtook the wind, and presently we passed
into a golden haze through which there loomed half-seen islands
with cities on their heights and palaces among leafy gardens.
Once a fallow doe fled past us, chased by a milk-white hound
with one blood-red ear; and once a maiden fled by on a bay
horse, and she carrying a golden apple in her hand, and close
behind her in hot pursuit, a young man on a white steed, a purple
and crimson cloak flying from his shoulders, and a great sword
naked in his hand.

"But the sky began to darken overhead, and the wind rose
and began to blow in great gusts that roused the waves to fury and
sent the spindrift flying like white birds over our heads, and the
lightning leapt between the dark sky and darker sea, while the
thunder boomed and crashed all about us. Yet still the white horse
sped on, unafraid, as lightly and sweetly as over the summer seas
that we had traversed before. And presently the wind died and

the darkness rolled away and sunshine touched the racing seas with gold. And ahead of us, under the spreading lake of blue sky, lay the fairest land that ever I had seen. Green plains and distant hills were all bathed in a honey-wash of sunlight that flashed and sparkled from the lakes and streams that met every turn of the eye, and changed to gold the white walls of the beautiful palace which stood close beside the shore. Flowers were everywhere, and butterflies like dancing flames upon the air, and as soon as I saw it, I knew that this could be no place but Tyr-na-nOg, the Land of Youth.

"The white horse skimmed the waves toward the shore, and on the white sand we dismounted, and Niamh turned to me, most sweetly holding out her hands, and said, 'This is my own land. Everything I promised, you shall find here, and above all and before all, the love of Niamh of the Golden Hair.'

"Then there came toward us from the palace a troop of warriors, heroes and champions all, holding their shields reversed in token to me that they came in peace. And after them a gay and beautiful company led by the King of the land himself, in a robe of yellow silk, a golden crown blazing like the midsummer sun upon his head. And behind him came the Queen, most fair to see, and with a hundred maidens clustered all about her.

"They kissed their daughter joyfully and tenderly, and the King took my hand in his saying, 'A hundred thousand welcomes, brave Oisin.' Then turning with me to face all the host, he said, 'This is Oisin, from the far-off land of Erin, he who is to be the husband of Niamh of the Golden Hair. Bid him welcome, as I do.'

"Then all the host, nobles and warriors and maidens alike bade me welcome. And all together, Niamh and myself walking hand in hand in their midst, we went up to the palace, where a great feast was prepared.

"For ten days and nights we feasted, while the harpers made

music sweeter than any heard in the world of men. I, Oisin, say that, I who was a harper among harpers of the world of men, in my time—and little birds as brightly colored as flowers flew and fluttered about the banquet house. And on the tenth day, Niamh and I were wed.

"I lived in the Land of Youth three years—I thought it was three years—and I was happy as never man was happy before. But as the third year drew to a close, I began to think more and more of my father and my son, and of all the companions of my youth. Sometimes as we rode hunting, I would fancy that I heard the Fian hunting horn echoing through the woods, and think I recognised the deep baying of Bran and Skolawn among the belling of the milk-white Danann hounds. I began to fall into waking dreams, thinking how they would be hunting the woods of Slieve Bloom, or how the heroes would be telling old stories about the fire, in Almu of the White Walls, until it came to this— that Niamh asked me if I no longer loved her. I told her that she was the very life of my heart, and that I was happy as ever I had been in the Land of Youth, but the restlessness was on me, and I longed to see my father and my friends once more.

"Then Niamh kissed me and clung to me, and tried to turn my thoughts elsewhere. But still I half-heard the Fian hunting horn echoing through my dreams at night, and at last I begged leave of her and of the King her father, to visit my own land once more.

"The King gave me leave, though unwillingly, and Niamh said, 'It's not that I can be holding you while your heart draws you back to Erin, so I give you my leave also, though there's a shadow on my mind, and I fear that I shall never see you again.'

"I said, 'That is a foolish fear, for there's nothing that could keep me long from you. Only give me the white steed, for he knows the way and will bring me back safely to your side.'

"Then she said, 'I will give you the white steed, for indeed he knows the way. But listen now, and keep my words in your mind. Never once dismount from his back all the while you are in the world of men, for if you do, you can never come back to me. If once your feet touch the green grass of Erin, the way back to Tyr-na-nOg will be closed to you forever.'

"I promised that I would never dismount from the white steed, but remember always her words. And seeing her grief, which even my most faithful promise seemed not to touch, I was within a featherweight of yielding to her and remaining always in Tyr-na-nOg; but the white horse stood ready, and the hunger was still on me, to see my father and my own land.

"So I mounted, and the horse set off at a gallop toward the shore. So again we sped across the sea, and the wind overtook the waves and we overtook the wind, and the shores of the Land of Youth sank into the golden mist behind us.

"Again it drifted all about us, that golden mist, and in the mist the towers and cities of the sea arose once more. And again the maiden with the golden apple in her hand fled past us on her bay horse, and the young horseman riding hard behind, his purple cloak streaming from his shoulders and his sword naked in his hand. And again the fallow doe fled by, hunted by the milk-white hound with one ear red as blood.

"So we came at last to the green shores of Erin.

"Gladly, once we were on land, I turned the horse's head toward Almu of the White Walls and rode on. And as I rode, I looked about me, seeking for familiar scenes and faces, and listening always for the sound of the Fian hunting horn. But all things seemed strangely altered, and nowhere did I hear or see any sign of my companions, and the folk who were tilling the ground were small and puny, so that they did not seem any more like countrymen of mine.

"I came at last through the woods to the open country around the Hill of Almu, and the hill was still there but overgrown with bushes and brambles, and on its broad flat crest, where the white walls of my father's dun had used to rise with its byres and barns and armorers' shops, the women's court and the guest quarters, and Finn's mighty mead-hall rising in the midst of all, were nothing but grassy hummocks grown over with elder and black-thorn and the arched sprays of the brambles, and the heather washing over all.

"Then horror fell upon me—though indeed I believed then that the dun was still there, but hidden from me by some enchant-ment of the Danann folk. And I flung wide my arms and shouted the names of Finn my father and Osca, and after them, the names of all the old brotherhood, Keelta, and Conan and Dering and the rest. Even Dearmid's name I shouted in that dreadful time. But no one answered, nothing moved save a thrush fluttering among the elder bushes. Then I thought that perhaps the hounds might hear me when men could not, and I shouted to Bran and Skolawn and strained my ears for an answering bark. But no sound came, save the hushing of a little wind through the hilltop grasses.

"So with the horror thick upon me, I wheeled the white horse and rode away from Almu, to search all Erin until I found my friends again, or some way out of the enchantment that held me captive. But everywhere I rode, I met only little puny people who gazed at me in wonder out of the faces of strangers, and in every household of the Fianna the brambles grew and the birds were at their nesting. So at last I came to the Glen of the Thrushes, where often I had hunted with Finn, and saw before me tilled land where I remembered only forest.

"And at the head of the tilled land a knot of these small and puny strangers were striving to shift a great stone that was in the way of the plowing. I rode closer, and they asked me for my help. And that was an easy thing to give, so I stooped in the saddle and set my hand under the stone and sent it rolling down the hillside. But with the strain of the heave my saddle girth broke, and I was flung to the ground, and my feet were on the green grass of Erin.

"Priest Patrick, the rest of my story they have told you!"

■ ■ ■

"You can't have living without dying," Angus Tuck tells Winnie. Angus Tuck, however, has never had to face death himself. Both writers of these poems were facing death. Do you think they might disagree with Tuck about the nature of death?

I Thought to Live
Hanabusa Ikkei

I thought to live	*Ni- sambyaku*
two centuries, or three—	*ikiyo to koso*
yet here comes death	*omoishi ni*
to me, a child	*hachijugo nite*
just eighty-five years old.	*fuji no wakajini*

Farewell
Hakusai

Farewell—and though there be	*Saraba saraba*
no budding in the spring,	*hana mo momiji mo*
no autumn withering—all is well.	*naki zo yoki*

■ ■ ■

The Water of Life, the Fountain of Youth, the magic spring—it seems as though you can't have immortality without a good water supply. This Water of Life works a little differently from Winnie Foster's magic spring.

The Water of Life
Howard Pyle

Once upon a time there was an old king who had a faithful servant. There was nobody in the whole world like him, and this was why: around his wrist he wore an armlet that fitted as close as the skin. There were words on the golden band; on one side they said:

"WHO THINKS TO WEAR ME ON HIS ARM
MUST LACK BOTH GUILE AND THOUGHT OF HARM."

And on the other side they said:

"I AM FOR ONLY ONE AND HE
SHALL BE AS STRONG AS TEN CAN BE."

At last the old king felt that his end was near, and he called the faithful servant to him and besought him to serve and aid the young king who was to come, as he had served and aided the old king who was to go. The faithful servant promised that which was asked, and then the old king closed his eyes and folded his hands and went the way that those had traveled who had gone before him.

Well, one day a stranger came to that town from over

the hills and far away. With him he brought a painted picture, but it was all covered with a curtain so that nobody could see what it was.

He drew aside the curtain and showed the picture to the young king, and it was a likeness of the most beautiful princess in the whole world; for her eyes were as black as a crow's wing, her cheeks were as red as apples, and her skin as white as snow. Moreover, the picture was so natural that it seemed as though it had nothing to do but to open its lips and speak.

The young king just sat and looked and looked. "Oh me!" said he, "I will never rest content until I have such a one as that for my own."

"Then listen!" said the stranger, "this is a likeness of the princess that lives over beyond the three rivers. Awhile ago she had a wise bird on which she doted, for it knew every-thing that happened in the world, so that it could tell the princess whatever she wanted to know. But now the bird is dead, and the princess does nothing but grieve for it day and night. She keeps the dead bird in a glass casket, and has promised to marry whoever will bring a cup of water from the Fountain of Life, so that the bird may be brought back to life again." That was the story the stranger told, and then he jogged on the way he was going, and I, for one, do not know whither it led.

But the young king had no peace or comfort in life for thinking of the princess who lived over beyond the three rivers. At last he called the faithful servant to him. "And can you not," said he, "get me a cup of the Water of Life?"

"I know not, but I will try," said the faithful servant, for he bore in mind what he had promised to the old king.

So out he went into the wide world, to seek for what the

young king wanted, though the way there is both rough and thorny. On he went and on, until his shoes were dusty, and his feet were sore, and after a while he came to the end of the earth, and there was nothing more over the hill. There he found a little tumbled-down hut, and within the hut sat an old, old woman with a distaff, spinning a lump of flax.

"Good-morning, mother," said the faithful servant.

"Good-morning, son," says the old woman, "and where are you traveling that you have come so far?"

"Oh!" says the faithful servant, "I am hunting for the Water of Life, and have come as far as this without finding a drop of it."

"Hoity, toity," says the old woman, "If that is what you are after, you have a long way to go yet. The fountain is in the country that lies east of the Sun and west of the Moon, and it is few that have gone there and come back again, I can tell you. Besides that, there is a great dragon that keeps watch over the water, and you will have to get the better of him before you can touch a drop of it. All the same, if you have made up your mind to go you may stay here until my sons come home, and perhaps they can put you in the way of getting there, for I am the Mother of the Four Winds of Heaven, and it is few places that they have not seen."

So the faithful servant came in and sat down by the fire to wait till the Winds came home.

The first that came was the East Wind; but he knew nothing of the Water of Life and the land that lay east of the Sun and west of the Moon; he had heard folks talk of them both now and then, but he had never seen them with his own eyes.

The next that came was the South Wind, but he knew no more of it than his brother, and neither did the West

Wind for the matter of that.

Last of all came the North Wind, and dear, dear, what a hubbub he made outside of the door, stamping the dust off of his feet before he came into the house.

"And do you know where the Fountain of Life is, and the country that lies east of the Sun and west of the Moon?" said the old woman.

Oh, yes, the North Wind knew where it was. He had been there once upon a time, but it was a long, long distance away.

"So, good! Then perhaps you will give this lad a lift over there tomorrow," said the old woman.

At this the North Wind grumbled and shook his head; but at last he said "yes," for he is a good-hearted fellow at bottom, is the North Wind, though his ways are a trifle rough perhaps.

So the next morning he took the faithful servant on his back, and away he flew till the man's hair whistled behind him. On they went and on they went and on they went, until at last they came to the country that lay east of the Sun and west of the Moon; and they were none too soon getting there either, I can tell you, for when the North Wind tumbled the faithful servant off his back he was so weak that he could not have lifted a feather.

"Thank you," said the faithful servant, and then he was for starting away to find what he came for.

"Stop a bit," says the North Wind, "you will be wanting to come away again after a while. I cannot wait here, for I have other business to look after. But here is a feather; when you want me, cast it into the air, and I will not be long in coming."

Then away he bustled, for he had caught his breath

again, and time was none too long for him.

The faithful servant walked along a great distance until, by and by, he came to a field covered all over with sharp rocks and white bones, for he was not the first by many who had been that way for a cup of the Water of Life.

There lay the great fiery dragon in the sun, sound asleep, and so the faithful servant had time to look about him. Not far away was a great deep trench like a drain in a swampy field; that was a path that the dragon had made by going to the river for a drink of water every day. The faithful servant dug a hole in the bottom of this trench, and there he hid himself as snugly as a cricket in the crack in the kitchen floor. By and by the dragon awoke and found that he was thirsty, and then started down to the river to get a drink. The faithful servant lay as still as a mouse until the dragon was just above where he was hidden, then he thrust his sword through its heart, and there it lay, after a turn or two, as dead as a stone.

After that he had only to fill the cup at the fountain, for there was nobody to say nay to him. Then he cast the feather into the air, and there was the North Wind, as fresh and as sound as ever. The North Wind took him upon its back, and away it flew until it came home again.

The faithful servant thanked them all around—the Four Winds and the old woman—and as they would take nothing else, he gave them a few drops of the Water of Life, and that is the reason that the Four Winds and their mother are as fresh and young now as they were when the world began.

Then the faithful servant set off home again, right foot foremost, and he was not as long in getting there as in coming.

As soon as the king saw the cup of the Water of Life he

had the horses saddled, and off he and the faithful servant rode to find the princess who lived over beyond the three rivers. By and by they came to the town, and there was the princess mourning and grieving over her bird just as she had done from the first. But when she heard that the king had brought the Water of Life she welcomed him as though he were a flower in March.

They sprinkled a few drops upon the dead bird, and up it sprang as lively and as well as ever.

But now, before the princess would marry the king she must have a talk with the bird, and there came the hitch, for the Wise Bird knew as well as you and I that it was not the king who had brought the Water of Life. "Go and tell him," said the Wise Bird, "that you are ready to marry him as soon as he saddles and bridles the Wild Black Horse in the forest over yonder, for if he is the hero who found the Water of Life he can do that, and more, easily enough."

The princess did as the bird told her, and so the king missed getting what he wanted after all. But off he went to the faithful servant. "And can you not saddle and bridle the Wild Black Horse for me?" said he.

"I do not know," said the faithful servant, "but I will try."

So off he went to the forest to hunt up the Wild Black Horse, the saddle over his shoulder and the bridle over his arm. By and by came the Wild Black Horse galloping through the woods like a thunder gust in summer, so that the ground shook under his feet. But the faithful servant was ready for him; he caught him by the mane and forelock, and the Wild Black Horse had never had such a one to catch hold of him before.

But how they did stamp and wrestle! Up and down and here and there, until the fire flew from the stones under their feet. But the Wild Black Horse could not stand against the strength of ten men, such as the faithful servant had, so by and by he fell on his knees, and the faithful servant clapped the saddle on his back and slipped the bridle over his ears.

"Listen now," says he; "tomorrow my master, the king, will ride you up to the princess's house, and if you do not do just as I tell you, it will be the worse for you; when the king mounts upon your back you must stagger and groan, as though you carried a mountain."

The horse promised to do as the other bade, and then the faithful servant jumped on his back and away to the king, who had been waiting at home for all this time.

The next day the king rode up to the princess's castle, and the Wild Black Horse did just as the faithful servant told him to do; he staggered and groaned, so that everybody cried out, "Look at the great hero riding upon the Wild Black Horse!"

And when the princess saw him she also thought that he was a great hero. But the Wise Bird was of a different mind from her, for when the princess came to talk to him about marrying the king he shook his head. "No, no," said he, "there is something wrong here, and the king has baked his cake in somebody else's oven. He never saddled and bridled the Wild Black Horse by himself. Listen, you must say to him that you will marry nobody but the man who wears such and such a golden armlet with this and that written on it."

So the princess told the king what the Wise Bird had bidden her to say, and the king went straightway to the faithful servant.

"You must let me have your armlet," said he.

"Alas, master," said the faithful servant, "that is a woeful thing for me, for the one and only way to take the armlet off of my wrist is to cut my hand from off my body."

"So!" says the king, "that is a great pity, but the princess will not have me without the armlet."

"Then you shall have it," says the faithful servant; but the king had to cut the hand off, for the faithful servant could not do it himself.

But, bless your heart! The armlet was ever so much too large for the king to wear! Nevertheless he tied it to his wrist with a bit of ribbon, and off he marched to the princess's castle.

"Here is the armlet of gold," said he, "and now will you marry me!"

But the Wise Bird sat on the princess's chair. "Hut! tut!" says he, "it does not fit the man."

Yes, that was so; everybody who was there could see it easily enough; and as for marrying him, the princess would marry nobody but the man who could wear the armlet.

What a hubbub there was then! Everyone who was there was sure that the armlet would fit him if it fitted nobody else. But no; it was far too large for the best of them. The faithful servant was very sad, and stood back of the rest, over by the wall, with his arm tied up in a napkin. "You shall try it too," says the princess; but the faithful servant only shook his head, for he could not try it on as the rest had done, because he had no hand. But the Wise Bird was there and knew what he was about. "See now," says he, "maybe the Water of Life will cure one thing as well as another."

Yes, that was true, and one was sent to fetch the cup. They sprinkled it on the faithful servant's arm, and it was not twice they had to do it, for there was another hand as good and better than the old.

Then they gave him the armlet; he slipped it over his hand, and it fitted him like his own skin.

"This is the man for me," says the princess, "and I will have none other"; for she could see with half an eye that he was the hero who had been doing all the wonderful things that had happened, because he said nothing about himself.

As for the king—why, all that was left for him to do was to pack off home again; and I, for one, am glad of it.

And this is true: the best packages are not always wrapped up in blue paper and tied with a gay string, and there are better men in the world than kings and princes, fine as they seem to be.

■　■　■

Isolation—the Tucks know it, and you've probably felt it too at one time or another. In this German legend, a man has to wander the seas alone because of terrible mistakes he has made in the past. Do you think this isolation is more punishment than he deserves, or has he gotten off too easily?

The Flying Dutchman
a German legend
retold by C. E. Smith

Many many years ago a Norwegian skipper named Daland was sailing homeward one evening after a long and successful voyage.

His heart was filled with longing for the sight of his only child, the beautiful dark-eyed Senta. And as he walked back and forward on the narrow deck of his swift sailing ship, he thought joyfully, 'To-night I shall be home, and shall hold in my arms once more, my beloved daughter.'

As night fell, the wind began to sing and hum among the snowy sails; dark clouds scudded across the starry sky, and every now and again heavy rain fell with a hissing noise on the deck.

'It is only a squall,' the captain shouted to his crew, 'and will go as suddenly as it has come.'

But by midnight the singing of the wind had risen to an angry shriek. The masts swayed and bent beneath the burden of the wind-filled sails, and huge waves crested with foam raced madly onward, lashed by the fury of the rising wind.

Daland soon knew that this was no passing squall, but a storm in which it would be dangerous if not impossible to sail past the rocky headland, beyond which lay the sandy bay he had hoped to reach that night. With a disappointed heart he gave orders that the sails should be closely reefed. He then altered the vessel's course and steered for the shelter of a rocky cove. Under its lee he could wait till the storm was past.

'Never do I remember a storm so sudden and so fierce,' he said to the sailors. 'Heaven help all those who are on the open sea this night.'

Scarcely had he spoken when a flash of lightning, closely followed by a loud peal of thunder, lit up for an instant the angry sea, and from the helmsman came the cry, 'Ship ahoy, ship ahoy!'

Daland rushed to his vessel's side and saw the lights of another ship entering the cove. He heard a clear voice of command ring from the stranger's deck. A heavy anchor was let down, and soon the newcomer swayed on the heaving waters close beside the Norwegian vessel. Worn and battered the stranger's ship appeared—a gloomy ship with blood-red sails, which the sailors were silently lowering.

No sound of voices was heard on board, no laughter to tell of rejoicing over deliverance from the terrors of the storm. In silence the vessel lay, and the Norwegian sailors, who had been eager to offer words of question and of welcome, turned away from a crew which appeared so unfriendly.

But presently the captain hailed Daland and invited him to come aboard, and in the stranger's cabin they spent the long night hours. Then, as the sun rose, the storm slowly died away.

'I have wandered much,' said the stranger to Daland, 'over unknown and distant seas. Wealth of gold and silver and pearls is mine safely hidden in secret coffers within these cabin walls. But now I long for rest and home. How gladly would I give half my treasure could I find a maiden who would love me truly, and be my wife. In Norway I mean to seek her, for they tell me that the maidens of Norway are loving and fair. What sayest thou who knowest them, noble Daland?'

Daland was greatly attracted by the stranger's noble look and manner. His face was very handsome, with delicate, clear-cut features that looked as if they were carved in ivory, so colourless was the skin. But it was the stranger's eyes that fascinated Daland most; dark, beautiful eyes that Daland felt were the saddest he had ever seen.

Daland's own eyes shone with eagerness when he heard of the treasures of gold and pearls hidden so close beside him, and his thoughts flew to Senta.

'It is not for me, noble stranger, to say whether our maidens are as thou believest, but I have a daughter at home, and if thou wilt come with me to-morrow, for thyself thou canst judge if she be fair, and well can I vouch that she is loving.'

The stranger readily agreed to sail with Daland next day, and they parted. But Daland could not sleep for thinking of the riches that might so soon be his. How often he had longed to find a noble and wealthy husband who would be worthy of Senta. Surely never had a storm brought such good fortune to any captain.

At sunrise the two ships weighed anchor, and in the golden light of dawn they left the shelter of the little cove, and steered for the rocky headland beyond which lay the sandy bay where Daland lived.

High on the rocky cliffs, which rose like a wall on two sides of the sandy bay, stood Daland's home. It was a low white house, standing back from the edge of the cliff in a garden, and well sheltered by the pine trees which clothed the steep hill slopes for many and many a mile.

Senta's mother had died when she was a baby, leaving

the little dark-eyed daughter to keep her memory green in the heart of her sailor husband. And Daland, as he looked now on his daughter, saw again the fair young maiden whom he had loved and wooed eighteen years ago. The love of both husband and father he now lavished on his child.

During his long absences at sea Dame Mary, his mother's old nurse, kept Senta company and looked after the house. In the long winter evenings the village maidens would gather in the big kitchen beside the open fireplace where pine logs blazed with a cheery sputter. Then, while their spinning wheels hummed busily, Dame Mary told tale after tale of fairy and witch and wanderer whose doings had been the delight of her own youthful days. Many a ballad she had taught to Senta.

'The child is over fond of these old-world songs,' she would say to Daland, half complainingly, 'and her wheel stands idle while she sings, which is not the way my mother taught me should the hours be spent.'

But the father always met these complaints with a smile.

'Let be, let be, Dame Mary,' he would say, 'Senta is still but a child. There will be time enough to spin when she has outgrown this love of childish tale and ballad.'

And indeed, few could have found it in their heart to scold the lovely, dream-eyed maiden. Except in song her voice was rarely heard, and her slender, graceful form moved silently about the house and garden. But Senta's favourite haunt was the edge of the rocky cliff at the foot of which rolled the sea.

Here she would sit hour after hour watching for the first glimpse of her father's ship, she told Dame Mary; for Senta knew that her old nurse would not understand if she spoke of the fascination which drew her again and again to watch the play of light and shadow on the face of the silent sea.

And when the storm winds blew, and the roar of the great

waves as they hurled themselves against the rocky cliffs was heard in the low white house in its sheltered garden, then the tumult of the wind and sea seemed to enter Senta's blood. She would roam from room to room in a fever of unrest, longing to be like the sea-gulls that floated on airy wings in the heart of the hurricane.

On the wall of the kitchen there hung a portrait which was noticed by every visitor and which Daland thought was strangely out of keeping with the simple furniture in the big old room. No one could be quite sure whence it had come; but Dame Mary, who knew most old tales connected with the family, believed that Daland's grandfather had brought it home as his share of the spoil from a wrecked ship that had drifted into the bay. 'And a sad-faced, wicked-looking man I think he is,' she used to add. 'I feel sure he has had dealings with the Evil One.' Then Dame Mary would make the sign of the cross and mutter a prayer that Heaven would keep her from such a sin.

But Senta loved the picture. To her the man's face was filled with deep sadness and longing without any sign of evil, and there welled up in her heart a great pity for the sorrow which was graven so deeply, and a longing that by her love she might in some way have lessened it.

Many a time when Dame Mary was busy at the other end of the house Senta would sit with folded hands gazing at the picture, her eyes filled with dreams. For long she had wondered what sorrow there could be so great as to bring that look of sadness into a man's face. But now she knew.

One wintry evening, when the storm raged more fiercely than usual, and shook the walls of the low white house, Dame Mary had told a tale of one whose face, Senta thought, might have looked like the portrait on the wall.

It was a tale of the sea, of a night of tempest and hurricane long, long ago, when a ship with close-reefed sails and anxious crew was struggling to round the Cape of Good Hope, that cape of storms so dreaded by all who sail the sea. Again and again the howling wind and the angry sea drove the vessel back, but with each defeat the captain's anger rose, and again he would renew his efforts to round the point. All night they battled, and when morning drew near a worn and weary sailor ventured to ask the captain, 'Shall we not give in and run for the shelter of the bay?'

But with blazing eyes and angry voice the captain shouted with a terrible oath, 'May I double the Cape this night even if afterwards I must sail for ever.'

And the wish was heard. An evil voice spoke mockingly in the captain's ear, 'In winter and summer, in storm and sunshine shalt thou sail, ever longing for rest, even the rest of death, and ever condemned to fare onward. Only one hope is thine. Each time that seven years pass thou mayst land, and shouldst thou find a maiden who will love thee unto death and join her lot with thine, then shalt thou be free.'

Many and many a time had the seven years' truce arrived, and with hopeful heart the captain had sought for the maiden who should free him from his fate, but the search had always been in vain.

By sailors the 'Flying Dutchman,' as the captain came to be called, was dreaded, as bad luck and storms were sure to follow in his track.

And so shunned by man, and under the curse of heaven, he wandered from age to age across the homeless sea.

Senta loved his tale better than all others, and in her heart she wished that hers had been the chance to offer her love and her life to save the wanderer.

But besides Dame Mary there was one who little liked the

maiden's dreamy fancies. Erick, the young huntsman, had loved Senta since they had played together as children. He was poor, and Daland, he knew, had higher hopes for the future of his only child than to wed her to a penniless hunter. But Senta liked well the handsome, fearless youth, and only three days before, Erick had drawn from her the avowal that no living person came nearer in her regard than he. Filled with hope, he now longed for Daland's home-coming that he might ask his leave to woo his daughter.

Great were the joy and excitement when word was brought that Daland's ship and another were entering the bay. The village maidens ran to the beach to welcome the travellers, while Senta and Dame Mary made ready a plentiful meal in the big old kitchen.

'Daughter, I bring thee a good friend whom I hope thou wilt heartily welcome,' was Daland's greeting to Senta as he clasped her in his arms.

And when Senta raised her head from her father's bosom the colour fled from her cheeks, and surprise and fear filled her heart. Before her there stood the living image of the portrait on the wall. The man with the saddest of sad faces was by her side, and a low, tired voice was begging for welcome.

'It seems to me as if I had known him all my life,' said Senta to Daland, giving her hand to the stranger, who gazed with eager eyes at the fair young face so steadfast and loving.

Right happy was the meal that sunny morning. Daland was overjoyed to be once more at home, and he had noticed with pleasure how heartily the shy Senta had welcomed his new friend.

'I shall let him tell his own tale,' he said to himself. 'With a young girl like Senta that handsome face will more quickly win approval than mention of gold or jewels.' And his eyes sparkled as he thought of the good fortune that lay before his child.

Dame Mary was always tearfully thankful to see her master safe home again. During her long life she had seen many ships sail bravely from the harbour away to the crimson west, but she could never forget that not always had they come back again, and the fishing village held many homes where wives and daughters mourned for those gone down in the great waters.

To the stranger the sight of this peaceful home life was like a glimpse of heaven, and as he looked on Senta's sweet face once more a gleam of hope stole into his heart, and he made up his mind to tell her his pitiful tale.

And for Senta the whole world thrilled with happiness. The hero of her dreams sat by her side, and she knew in her heart that behind the beautiful face of her father's guest lay hidden a depth of sorrow which she alone could sound.

In the garden, alone with the stranger, she listened while he told the tale of his weary wanderings under the evil spirit's curse, and his voice faltered as he said, 'Senta, couldest thou love me with a love faithful even unto death, that deliverance might be mine?'

And the sadness in his face gave place to a look of joy and hope as the maiden answered, 'I have loved thee for long with the strongest love of my heart, and faithfully will I follow thee even unto death.'

By evening it was known in all the village that Senta was betrothed to the captain of the stranger ship, and that Daland had found a noble and wealthy son-in-law for his only child. By his orders the villagers carried food and wine to the sailors of both ships, that they might feast and drink good luck to the coming bridal.

With right goodwill the men on Daland's ship made merry, and sounds of song and laughter floated across the bay. But presently it was noticed that silence reigned among the stranger crew. Not a rope was moved, not a voice was heard till after the sun had set. Then strange mutterings as of a coming storm filled the air; the blood-red sails of the gloomy ship fluttered as with wind in the still evening, and blue flames were seen to flicker round the bows of the mysterious vessel. No sailors were seen, but harsh voices sang songs of murder and hate and wickedness, while hideous laughter followed each cruel verse.

The sailors in Daland's ship grew silent, and fear struck a chill to their hearts.

'I know that ship,' whispered an old sailor, who had come from the village to welcome his grandson; 'it is the Flying Dutchman, and her captain and crew are under the power of the Evil One. God send that no ill-gotten treasure will tempt Daland to give his daughter to one so doomed.' And the sailors crossed themselves and went below in fear.

Erick the huntsman, who had been on the hills all day, and had just come on board to join the merry-makers, heard all that was said by the old sailor. In great misery he went ashore to seek for Daland, and warn him of the true nature of his guest.

On the cliffs he saw Senta gazing seaward with dreamy, unseeing eyes.

'Is it true, Senta,' he asked, 'that thou hast promised to marry the stranger captain?'

'Erick, it had to be,' answered Senta. 'All my life have I been waiting for him, and now my heart calls me to follow him throughout the world.'

'And what of thy promise to me, false maiden?' burst from Erick angrily. 'Knowest thou that this man is under a curse, and that earth and sea alike refuse shelter to him who hath made a vow to the Evil One? Thy love is mine! But three days have passed since thou toldest me that no living person came nearer to thy heart than I. As my promised bride I claim thee now.'

Erick seized Senta's hands to draw her to him. As he did so a dark shadow came from a corner of the rocky cliff, and a voice of deepest sadness was heard to say, 'Thou too art false, and I am lost, lost, lost.'

It was the voice of the stranger, who now ran down to the beach calling, 'To ship, to ship! Once more to sea we go!' and as the captain sprang on board, the blood-red sails of the gloomy boat were hoisted by the ghostly crew, and the vessel put out to sea.

Senta stood for a minute, spellbound by the stranger's sad words, then she cried, 'Stay, O stay! I am thine and thine only, I will go with thee even unto death!'

But the captain heard her not, already the blood-red sails of the ship were stiffening to the breeze, and the white foam flew from the vessel's bow.

Senta cast a farewell look at the low white house and garden, and at the brave young huntsman lover who stood by her side. Then she ran along the cliff to where it overhung the sea, and crying, 'I come, I come!' she threw herself down into the restless waves.

As she fell a beam of light shot from the rosy clouds which still lingered in the sunset sky, and those who were watching saw the vessel disappear, while the forms of Senta and the Flying Dutchman, with hands closely clasped, ascended on the golden pathway towards the glories of the West.

And all knew that Senta's faithful love had set the wanderer free, and he might now find rest.

■ ■ ■

Natalie Babbitt

■ (Born 1932) ■

Natalie Babbitt was born in Dayton, Ohio, on July 28, 1932. Her mother was a talented painter who encouraged Babbitt's interest in art. As a child, Babbitt loved to read, especially fairy tales and myths, and soon decided that she wanted to illustrate books for children.

At first, Babbitt had no interest in writing. While she was a student at Laurel School in Cleveland and at Smith College, she developed her skills as an artist. After completing her studies, she married Samuel Fisher Babbitt. They spent the next ten years raising their three children to school age while living in Connecticut, Tennessee, and Washington, D.C.

Just before Natalie and Samuel Babbitt moved to New York, they began writing a children's book together. After the move, however, Babbitt found herself writing alone because of Samuel's busy schedule as the president of Kirkland College. Her love for writing quickly grew, and she found that writing was far more important to her than illustrating. Babbitt still enjoys illustrating, but is better known for her fiction and poetry.

Babbitt has said that she finds it interesting that a single character in a story can mean so many different things to different people. She believes that each reader has a different background and personal history, which she calls a "filter," that he or she brings to the story. Therefore, one reader's understanding of the characters will be slightly different from another's. Babbitt enjoys writing stories in which the characters respond to situations in unusual ways because they see their circumstances through their own "filters."

Besides *Tuck Everlasting*, Natalie Babbitt has written several novels, including *Kneeknock Rise, Goody Hall,* and *Herbert Rowbarge.* She has also written two books of verse, *Dick Foote and the Shark* and *Phoebe's Revolt,* and two collections of short stories, *The Devil's Storybook* and *The Devil's Other Storybook.* In addition to writing, Babbitt has illustrated all of her own books and several books by other authors, including her husband Samuel Babbitt and the poet Valerie Worth.